JOAN AIKEN was born in Sussex in 1924 to
a family of writers. She had a variety of jobs,
including working for the BBC, the United
Nations Information Centre and as features
editor for a short story magazine before her
first children's novel, *The Kingdom and the
Cave*, was published in 1960. She wrote more
than a hundred books for young readers and
adults, and is recognized as one of the classic
authors of the twentieth century. Her books
are internationally acclaimed and she received
the Edgar Allan Poe Award in the United
States as well as the Guardian Award for
Fiction in this country for *The Whispering
Mountain*. In 1999 she was awarded the
MBE for her services to literature. Joan
Aiken died in 2004.

Books by Joan Aiken

The Wolves of Willoughby Chase sequence

THE WHISPERING MOUNTAIN
THE WOLVES OF WILLOUGHBY CHASE
BLACK HEARTS IN BATTERSEA
NIGHT BIRDS ON NANTUCKET
THE STOLEN LAKE
LIMBO LODGE
THE CUCKOO TREE
DIDO AND PA
IS
COLD SHOULDER ROAD
MIDWINTER NIGHTINGALE
THE WITCH OF CLATTERINGSHAWS

See all books at joanaiken.com

JOAN AIKEN

ARABEL AND MORTIMER STORIES

Illustrated by Quentin Blake

A PUFFIN BOOK

PUFFIN BOOKS

UK | USA | Canada | Ireland | Australia
India | New Zealand | South Africa

Puffin Books is part of the Penguin Random House group of companies
whose addresses can be found at global.penguinrandomhouse.com.

www.penguin.co.uk
www.puffin.co.uk
www.ladybird.co.uk

The stories in this collection were first published as follows:
'Arabel's Raven' © 1972
'The Escaped Black Mamba' © 1973
'The Bread Bin' © 1974
'Mortimer's Tie' © 1976
'The Spiral Stair' © 1979
'Mortimer and the Sword Excalibur' © 1979

Set in 12.5/16.5 pt Sabon LT Std
Typeset by Jouve (UK), Milton Keynes
Printed and bound in Great Britain by Clays Ltd, Elcograf S.p.A.

A CIP catalogue record for this book is available from the British Library

ISBN: 978-0-241-38657-6

All correspondence to:
Puffin Books
Penguin Random House Children's
80 Strand, London WC2R ORL

MIX
Paper from
responsible sources
FSC® C018179

Penguin Random House is committed to a
sustainable future for our business, our readers
and our planet. This book is made from Forest
Stewardship Council® certified paper.

Contents

Arabel's Raven   1

The Escaped Black Mamba   57

The Bread Bin   105

Mortimer's Tie   159

The Spiral Stair   231

Mortimer and the Sword Excalibur   285

Arabel's Raven

ON A STORMY night in March, not long ago, a respectable taxi driver named Ebenezer Jones found himself driving home, very late, through the somewhat wild and sinister district of London known as Rumbury Town. Mr Jones had left Rumbury Tube Station behind him, and was passing the long, desolate piece of land called Rumbury Waste, when, in the street not far ahead, he observed a large, dark, upright object. It was rather smaller than a coal hod, but bigger than a quart cider bottle, and it was moving slowly from one side of the street to the other.

Mr Jones had approached to within about twenty yards of this object when a motorbike with two riders shot by him, going at a reckless pace and cutting in very close. Mr Jones braked sharply,

looking in his rear-view mirror. When he looked
forward again he saw that the motorbike must
have struck the upright object in passing, for it was
now lying on its side, just ahead of his front wheels.

He brought his taxi to a halt.

'Not but what I daresay I'm being foolish,' he
thought. 'There's plenty in this part of town that's
best left alone. But you can't see something like
that happen without stopping to have a look.'

He got out of his cab.

What he found in the road was a large black
bird, almost two feet long, with a hairy fringe
round its beak. At first he thought it was dead.
But as he got nearer, it opened one eye slightly,
then shut it again.

'Poor thing; it's probably stunned,' thought
Mr Jones.

His horoscope in the *Hackney Drivers' Herald*
that morning had said: 'Due to your skill a life will
be saved today.' Mr Jones had been worrying, as he
drove home, because up till now he had not, so far
as he knew, saved any lives that day, except by
avoiding pedestrians recklessly crossing the road
without looking.

'This'll be the life I'm due to save,' he thought.
'Must be, for it's five to midnight now,' and he
went back to his cab for the bottle of brandy and

teaspoon he always carried in the tool kit in case lady passengers turned faint.

It is not at all easy to give brandy to a large bird lying unconscious in the road. After five minutes there was a good deal of brandy on the cobbles, and some up Mr Jones's sleeve, and some in his shoes, but he could not be sure that any had actually gone down the bird's throat. The difficulty was that he needed at least three hands: one to hold the bottle, one to hold the spoon, and one to hold the bird's beak open. If he prised open the beak with the handle of the teaspoon, it was sure to shut again before he had time to reverse the spoon and tip in some brandy.

Suddenly a hand fell on Mr Jones's shoulder.

'Just what do you think you're doing?' enquired one of two policemen who had left their van and were standing over him.

The other sniffed in a disapproving manner.

Mr Jones straightened slowly.

'I was just giving some brandy to this rook,' he explained. He was rather embarrassed, because he had spilt such a lot of the brandy.

'Rook? That's no rook,' said the officer who had sniffed. 'That's a raven. Look at its hairy beak.'

'Whatever it is, it's stunned,' said Mr Jones. 'A motorbike hit it.'

'Ah,' said the second officer, 'that'll have been one of the pair who just pinched thirty thousand quid from the bank in the High Street. It's the Cash-and-Carat boys – the ones who've done a lot of burglaries around here lately. Did you see which way they went?'

'No,' said Mr Jones, tipping up the raven's head, 'but they'll have a dent on their motorbike. Could one of you hold the bottle for me?'

'You don't want to give him brandy. Hot sweet tea's what you want to give him.'

'That's right,' said the other policeman. 'And an ice pack under the back of his neck.'

'Burn feathers in front of his beak.'

'Slap his hands.'

'Undo his shoelaces.'

'Put him in the fridge.'

'He hasn't got any shoelaces,' said Mr Jones, not best pleased at all this advice. 'If you aren't going to hold the bottle, why don't you go on and catch the blokes that knocked him over?'

'Oh, *they*'ll be well away by now. Besides, they carry guns. We'll go back to the station,' said the first policeman. 'And you'd better not stay here, giving intoxicating liquor to a bird, or we might have to take you in for loitering in a suspicious manner.'

'I can't just leave the bird here in the road,' said Mr Jones.

'Take it with you, then.'

'Can't you take it to the station?'

'Not likely,' said the second policeman. 'No facilities for ravens there.'

They stood with folded arms, watching, while Mr Jones slowly picked up the bird (it weighed about as much as a fox terrier) and put it in his taxi. And they were still watching as he started up and drove off.

So that was how Mr Jones happened to take the raven back with him to Number Six, Rainwater Crescent, London NW 3½, on a windy March night.

When he got home, nobody was up, which was not surprising, since it was after midnight.

He would have liked to wake his daughter, Arabel, who was fond of birds and animals. But since she was quite young – she hadn't started school yet – he thought he had better not. And he knew he must not wake his wife, Martha because she had to be at work, at Round & Round, the record shop in the High Street, at nine in the morning.

He laid the raven on the kitchen floor, opened the window to give it air, put on the kettle for hot sweet tea, and, while he had the match lit, burned a feather duster under the raven's beak. Nothing happened, except that the smoke made Mr Jones cough. He saw no way of slapping the raven's hands or undoing its shoelaces, so he took some ice cubes and a jug of milk from the fridge. He left the fridge door open because his hands were full, and anyway, it usually swung shut by itself.

With great care he slid a little row of ice cubes under the back of the raven's neck.

The kettle boiled and he made the tea: a spoonful for each person and one for the pot, three in all. He also spread himself a slice of bread and fish paste because he didn't see why he shouldn't have a little something as well as the bird. He poured out a cup of tea for himself and an egg-cup for the raven, putting plenty of sugar in both.

But when he turned round, egg-cup in hand, the raven had gone.

'Bless me,' Mr Jones said. 'There's ingratitude for you! After all my trouble! I suppose he flew out the window; those ice cubes certainly did the trick quick. I wonder if it would be a good notion to carry some ice cubes with me in the cab? I could put them in a vacuum flask – might be better than brandy if lady passengers turn faint . . .'

Thinking these thoughts he finished his tea (and the raven's; no sense in leaving it to get cold), turned out the light, and went to bed.

In the middle of the night he thought, 'Did I put the milk back in the fridge?'

And he thought, 'No, I didn't.'

And he thought, 'I ought to get up and put it away.'

And he thought, 'It's a cold night, the milk's not going to turn between now and breakfast. Besides, Thursday tomorrow, it's my early day.'

So he rolled over and went to sleep.

Every Thursday Mr Jones drove the local fishmonger, Mr Finney, over to Colchester to buy oysters at five in the morning. So, early next day, up he got, off he went. Made himself a cup of tea, finished the milk in the jug, never looked in the fridge.

An hour after he had gone, Mrs Jones got up and put on the kettle. Finding the milk jug empty she went yawning to the fridge and pulled the door open, not noticing that it had been prevented from shutting properly by the handle of a burnt feather duster which had fallen against the hinge. But she noticed what was inside the fridge all right. She let out a shriek that brought Arabel running downstairs.

Arabel was little and fair with grey eyes. She was wearing a white nightdress that made her look like a lampshade with two feet sticking out from the bottom. One of the feet had a blue sock on.

'What's the matter, Ma?' she said.

'There's a great awful *bird* in the fridge!' sobbed Mrs Jones. 'And it's eaten all the cheese and a blackcurrant tart and five pints of milk and a bowl of dripping and a pound of sausages. All that's left is the lettuce.'

'Then we'll have lettuce for breakfast,' said Arabel. But Mrs Jones said she didn't fancy lettuce that had spent the night in the fridge with a great awful bird.

'And how are we going to get it out of there?'

'The lettuce?'

'The *bird*!' said Mrs Jones, switching off the kettle and pouring hot water into a pot without any tea in it.

Arabel opened the fridge door, which had swung shut. There sat the bird, among the empty milk bottles, but he was a lot bigger than they were. There was a certain amount of wreckage

around him – torn foil, and cheese wrappings, and milk splashes, and bits of pastry, and crumbs of dripping, and rejected lettuce leaves. It was like Rumbury Waste after a picnic Sunday.

Arabel looked at the raven, and he looked back at her.

'His name's Mortimer,' she said.

'No, it's not, no, it's not!' cried Mrs Jones, taking a loaf from the bread bin and absent-mindedly running the tap over it. 'We said you could have a hamster when you were five, or a puppy or a kitten when you were six, and of course call it what you wish. Oh my *stars*, look at that creature's toenails, if nails they can be called, but not a bird like that, a great hairy awful thing eating us out of house and home, as big as a fire extinguisher and all the colour of a charcoal biscuit –'

But Arabel was looking at the raven and he was looking back at her.

'His name's Mortimer,' she said. And she put both arms round the raven, not an easy thing to do, all jammed in among the milk bottles as he was, and lifted him out.

'He's very heavy,' she said, and set him down on the kitchen floor.

'So I should think, considering he's got a pound of sausages, a bowl of dripping, five pints of milk, half a pound of New Zealand cheddar, and a blackcurrant tart inside him,' said Mrs Jones. 'I'll open the window. Perhaps he'll fly out.'

She opened the window. But Mortimer did not fly out. He was busy examining everything in the kitchen very thoroughly. He tapped the table legs with his beak – they were metal and clinked. Then he took everything out of the waste bin – a pound of peanut shells, two empty tins, and some jam tart cases. He particularly liked the jam tart cases, which he pushed under the lino. Then he walked over to the fireplace – it was an old-fashioned kitchen – and began chipping out the

mortar from between the bricks. Mrs Jones had been gazing at the raven as if she were under a spell, but when he began on the fireplace, she said,

'*Don't* let him do that!'

'Mortimer,' said Arabel, 'we'd like you not to do that, please.'

Mortimer turned his head right round on its black feathery neck and gave Arabel a thoughtful, considering look. Then he made his first remark, which was a deep, hoarse, rasping croak.

'Kaarrk.'

It said, as plainly as words: 'Well, all right, I won't do it this time, but I make no promise that I won't do it *some* time. And I think you are being unreasonable.'

'Wouldn't you like to see the rest of the house, Mortimer?' said Arabel. And she held open the kitchen door. Mortimer walked – he never hopped – very slowly through into the hall and looked at the stairs. They seemed to interest him greatly. He began going up them hand over hand – or, rather, beak over claw.

When he was halfway up, the telephone rang. It stood on the windowsill at the foot of the stairs, and Mortimer watched as Mrs Jones came to answer it.

Mr Jones was ringing from Colchester to ask if his wife wanted any oysters.

'Oysters!' she said. 'That bird you left in the fridge has eaten sausages, cheese, dripping, blackcurrant tart, drunk five pints of milk, now he's chewing the stairs, and you ask if I want oysters? Perhaps I should feed him caviare as well?'

'Bird I left in the fridge?' Mr Jones was puzzled. 'What bird, Martha?'

'That great black crow, or whatever it is. Arabel calls it Mortimer and she's leading it all over the house and now it's taken all the spools of thread from my sewing drawer and is pushing them under the doormat.'

'Not *it*, Ma. *He*. Mortimer,' said Arabel, going to open the front door and take the letters from the postman. But Mortimer got there first and received the letters in his beak.

The postman was so startled that he dropped his whole sack of post in a puddle and gasped, 'Nevermore will I stay later than half-past ten at the Oddfellows Ball or touch a drop stronger than Caribbean lemon, *nevermore*!'

'Nevermore,' said Mortimer, pushing two bills and a postcard under the door mat. Then he retrieved the postcard again by spearing it clean through the middle. Mrs Jones let out a wail.

'Arabel, *will* you come in out of the street in your nightie! Look what that bird's done, chewing

They had baked beans for lunch. Mortimer enjoyed the baked beans, but his table manners were very light-hearted. He liked knocking spoons and forks off the table, pushing them under the rush matting, and fetching them out again with a lot of excitement. Granny wasn't so keen on this.

While Granny was having her nap Arabel looked at comics and Mortimer looked at the stairs. There seemed to be something about stairs that appealed to him.

When Mr Jones came home at teatime the first thing he said was:

'What's happened to the three bottom steps?'

'What has, then?' asked Granny who was short-sighted and anyway busy spreading jam.

'They aren't there.'

'It wasn't Mortimer's fault,' said Arabel. 'He didn't know we need the stairs.'

'Mortimer? Who's Mortimer?'

Just then Mrs Jones came home.

'That bird has got to go,' said Mr Jones accusingly the minute she had put down her shopping basket and taken off her coat.

'Who's talking? *You* were the one who left him in the fridge.'

Mortimer looked morose and sulky at Mr Jones's words. He sank his head between his shoulders and ruffled up the beard round his beak and turned his toes in, as if he did not care one way or the other. But Arabel went so white that her father thought she was going to faint.

'If Mortimer goes,' she said, 'I shall cry *all* the time. Very likely I shall die!'

'Oh well . . .' said Mr Jones. 'But mind, if he stays, he's not to eat any more stairs!'

Just the same, during the next week or so, Mortimer did chew up six more stairs. The family had to go to bed by climbing a ladder. Luckily it was an aluminium fruit ladder, or Mortimer would probably have chewed that up too; he was very fond of wood.

There was a bit of trouble because he wanted to sleep in the fridge every night, but Mrs Jones put a stop to that; in the end he agreed to sleep in the airing cupboard. Then there was a bit more trouble because he pushed all the soap and toothbrushes under the bathroom lino and they couldn't get the door open. The fire brigade had to climb through the window.

'He's not to be left alone in the house,' Mr Jones said. 'On the days when Arabel goes to playgroup, Martha, he'll have to go to work with you.'

'Why can't he come to playgroup with me?' Arabel asked.

Mr Jones just laughed at that question.

Mrs Jones was not enthusiastic about taking Mortimer to work with her.

'So I'm to pull him up the High Street on that red truck? You must be joking.'

'He can ride on your shopping bag on wheels,' Arabel said. 'He'll like that.'

At first the owners of the record shop, Mr Round and Mr Toby Round, were quite pleased to have Mortimer sitting on the counter. People who lived in Rumbury Town heard about the raven in the record shop; they came in out of curiosity, and then they played records, and then, as often as not, bought them. And at first Mortimer was so astonished at the music that he sat still on the counter for hours at a time looking like a stuffed bird. At teatime, when Arabel came home from playgroup, she told him what she had been doing and pulled him around on the red truck.

But presently Mortimer became bored by just sitting listening to music. There was a telephone on the counter. One day when it rang Mrs Jones was wrapping up a record for a customer, so Mortimer got there first.

'Can you tell me the name of the new Weevils' LP?' said a voice.

'Nevermore!' said Mortimer.

Then he began taking triangular bites out of the edges of records. After that it wasn't so easy to sell them. Then he noticed the spiral stairs which led down to the classic and folk departments. One morning Mr Round and Mr Toby Round and Mrs Jones were all very busy arranging a display of new issues in the shop window. When they had finished they discovered that Mortimer had eaten the spiral staircase.

'Mrs Jones, you and your bird will have to go. We have kind, long-suffering natures, but Mortimer has done eight hundred and seventeen pounds, sixty-seven new pence' worth of damage. You may have a year to repay it. Please don't trouble to come in for the rest of the week.'

'Glad I am *I* haven't such a kind, long-suffering nature,' snapped Mrs Jones, and she dumped Mortimer on top of her wheeled shopping bag and dragged him home.

up the gas bill. Nevermore, indeed! I should just about say it *was* nevermore. No, I don't want any oysters, Ebenezer Jones, and please shut the front door, and *stop* that bird from pushing all those plastic flowers under the stair-carpet.'

Mr Jones couldn't understand all this, so he rang off. Five minutes later the telephone rang again. This time it was Mrs Jones's sister Brenda, to ask if Martha would like to come to play bingo that evening. But this time Mortimer got to the phone first; he picked up the receiver with his claw, exactly as he had seen Mrs Jones do, delivered a loud clicking noise into it – *click* – and said,

'Nevermore!'

Then he replaced the receiver.

'My goodness!' Brenda said to her husband. 'Ben and Martha must have had a terrible quarrel; he answered the phone and he didn't sound a *bit* like himself!'

Meanwhile, Mortimer had climbed upstairs and was in the bathroom trying the taps; it took him less than five minutes to work out how to turn them on. He liked to watch the cold water running, but the hot, with its clouds of steam, for some reason annoyed him, and he began throwing things at the hot tap: bits of soap, sponges, nail brushes, face flannels.

They choked up the plug hole and within a short time the water had overflowed and was flooding the bathroom.

'Mortimer, I think you'd better not stay in the bathroom,' Arabel said.

Mortimer was good at giving black looks; now he gave Arabel a black look. But she took no notice.

She had a red truck, which had once been filled with wooden building bricks. The bricks had been lost long ago, but the truck was in good repair.

'Mortimer, wouldn't you like a ride in this red truck?'

Mortimer thought he would. He climbed into the truck and stood there, waiting.

When Mrs Jones discovered Arabel pulling Mortimer along on the truck she nearly had a fit.

'It's not bad enough that you've adopted that big, ugly, sulky bird, but you have to pull him along on a *truck*? Don't his legs work? Why can't he walk, may I ask?'

'He doesn't feel like walking just now,' Arabel said.

'Of course! And I suppose he's *forgotten* how to *fly*?'

'I like pulling him on the truck,' Arabel said, and she pulled him into the garden. Presently Mrs Jones went off to work at Round & Round, the record shop, and Granny came in to look after Arabel. All Granny ever did was sit and knit. She liked answering the phone too, but now every time it rang Mortimer got there first, picked up the receiver, and said,

'Nevermore!'

People who rang up to order taxis were puzzled and said to one another, 'Mr Jones must have retired.'

'Stairs!' she said to Arabel. 'What's the use of a bird who eats stairs? Gracious knows there's enough rubbish in the world – why can't he eat plastic bottles, or ice-cream cartons, or used cars, or oil slicks, tell me that? But no! He has to eat the only thing that joins the upstairs to the downstairs.'

'Nevermore,' said Mortimer.

'Tell that to the space cavalry!' said Mrs Jones.

Arabel and Mortimer went and sat side by side on the bottom rung of the fruit ladder leaning against one another and very quiet.

'When I'm grown up,' Arabel said to Mortimer, 'we'll live in a house with a hundred stairs and you can eat them all.'

Meanwhile, since the bank raid on the night when Mr Jones had found Mortimer, several more places in Rumbury Town had been burgled: Brown's the ironmonger's, and Mr Finney the fishmonger, and the Tutti-Frutti Candy Shoppe.

On the day after Mrs Jones left Round & Round, she found another job, at Peter Stone, the jeweller's, in the High Street. She had to take both Arabel and Mortimer with her to work, since playgroup was finished until after Easter, and Granny had gone to Southend on a visit. Arabel pulled Mortimer to the shop every day on the red truck. Peter Stone, had no objection.

'The more people in the shop, the less chance of a hold-up,' he said. 'Too much we're hearing about these Cash-and-Carat boys for my taste. Raided the supermarket yesterday, they did; took a thousand tins of Best Jamaica blend coffee as the cash register was jammed. Coffee? What would they want with a thousand tins?'

'Perhaps they were thirsty,' Arabel said. She and Mortimer were looking at their reflections in a glass case full of bracelets. Mortimer tapped the glass in an experimental way with his beak.

'That bird, now,' Peter Stone said, giving Mortimer a thoughtful look. 'He'll behave himself? He won't go swallowing any diamonds? The brooch he's looking at now is worth forty thousand pounds.'

Mrs Jones drew herself up. 'Behave himself? Naturally he'll behave himself,' she said. 'Any diamonds he swallows I guarantee to replace!'

A police sergeant came into the shop. 'I've a message for your husband,' he said to Mrs Jones. 'We've found a motorbike, and we'd be glad if he'd step up to the station and say if he can identify it as the one that passed him the night the bank was robbed.' Then he saw Mortimer. 'Is that the bird that got knocked over? *He*'d better come along as well; we can see if he fits the dent in the petrol tank.'

'Nevermore,' said Mortimer, who was eyeing a large clock under a glass dome.

'He'd better not talk like that to the Super,' the sergeant said, 'or he'll be charged with obstructing the police.'

'Have they got any theories about the identity of the gang?' Peter Stone asked.

'No, they always wear masks. But we're pretty sure they're locals and have a hideout somewhere in the district, because we always lose track of them so fast. One odd feature is that they have a small accomplice, about the size of that bird there,' the sergeant said, giving Mortimer a hard stare.

'How do you know?'

'When they robbed the supermarket, someone got in through the manager's cat-door and opened a window from inside. If birds had fingerprints,' the sergeant said, 'I wouldn't mind taking the prints of that shifty-looking fowl. *He* could get through a cat flap, easy enough.'

'Your opinions are uncalled for,' said Mrs Jones. 'Thoughtless our Mortimer may be, untidy at times, but honest as a Bath bun, I'll have you know. And the night the supermarket was robbed he was in our airing cupboard with his head tucked under his wing.'

'I've known some Bath buns not all they should be,' said the sergeant.

'Kaark,' said Mortimer.

Five minutes after the sergeant had gone, Peter Stone went off for his lunch.

And five minutes after *that*, two masked men walked into the shop.

One of them pointed a gun at Mrs Jones and Arabel, the other smashed a glass case and took out the diamond brooch which Peter Stone had said was worth forty thousand pounds.

Out of the gunman's pocket clambered a grey
squirrel with an extremely villainous expression.
It looked hopefully round the shop.

'Piece of apple pie, this job,' said the masked
man who had taken the diamond brooch. 'We'll
give Sam the brooch and he can use the bird to
hitch a ride to our pad. Then if the caps should
stop us, they can't pin anything on us.'

Mortimer, who was eating one of the cheese
sandwiches Mrs Jones had brought for her lunch,
suddenly found a gun jammed against his ribs.
The squirrel jumped on his back.

'You'd better co-operate, Coal-face,' the gunman
said. 'This is a flyjack. Fly where Sam tells you, or

you'll be blown to forty bits. Sam carries a bomb round his neck on a shoelace; all he has to do is pull out the pin with his teeth.'

'Oh, please don't blow up Mortimer,' Arabel said to the gunman. 'I think he's forgotten how to fly.'

'He'd better remember pretty fast.'

'Oh dear, Mortimer, perhaps you'd better do what they say.'

With a creak that could be heard all over the jeweller's shop, Mortimer unfolded his wings and, to his own surprise as much as anyone else's, flew out through the open door with Sam sitting on his back. The two thieves walked calmly after him.

As soon as they were gone, Mrs Jones went into hysterics, and Arabel rang the alarm buzzer.

In no time a police-van bounced to a stop outside, with siren screaming and lights flashing. Peter Stone came rushing back from the Fish Bar.

Mrs Jones was still having hysterics, but Arabel said, 'Two masked gunmen stole a diamond brooch and gave it to a squirrel to carry away and he's flown off on our raven. Please get him back!'

'Where did the two men go?'

'They just walked off up the High Street.'

'All sounds like a fishy tale to me,' said the police sergeant – it was the same one who had been in earlier. 'You sure you didn't just give the brooch to the bird and tell him to flit off with it to the nearest stolen-property dealer?'

'Oh, how could you say such a thing,' wept Mrs Jones, 'when our Mortimer's the best-hearted raven in Rumbury Town, even if he does look a bit sulky at times?'

'Any clues?' said the sergeant to his men.

'There's a trail of cheese crumbs here,' said a constable. 'We'll see how far we can follow them.'

The police left, following the trail of cheese, which led all the way up Rumbury High Street, past the bank, past the fishmonger, past the supermarket, past the ironmonger, past the record shop, past the war memorial, and stopped at the tube station.

'He's done us,' said the sergeant. 'Went on by train. Did a large black bird buy a ticket to anywhere about ten minutes ago?' he asked Mr Gumbrell, the ticket clerk.

'No.'

'He could have got a ticket from a machine,' one of the constables pointed out.

'They all say "Out of Order".'

'Anyway, why should a bird buy a ticket? He could just fly into a train,' said another constable.

All the passengers who had travelled on the Rumberloo line that morning were asked if they had seen a large black bird or a squirrel carrying a diamond brooch. None of them had.

'No offence, Mrs Jones,' said Peter Stone, 'but in these doubtful circumstances I'd just as soon you didn't come back after lunch. We'll say nothing about the forty thousand pounds for the brooch at present. Let's hope the bird is caught with it on him.'

'He didn't take it,' said Arabel. 'You'll find out.'

Arabel and Mrs Jones walked home to Number Six, Rainwater Crescent. Arabel was pale and silent, but Mrs Jones scolded all the way.

'Any bird with a scrap of gumption would have taken the brooch off that wretched little rat of a squirrel. Ashamed of himself, he ought to be! Nothing but trouble and aggravation we've had since Mortimer has been in the family; let's hope that's the last of him.'

Arabel said she didn't want any tea, and went to bed, and cried herself to sleep.

That evening Mr Jones went up to the police station and identified the motorbike as the one that had passed him the night the bank had been robbed.

'Good,' said the sergeant. 'We found a couple of black feathers stuck to a bit of grease on the tank. If you ask *me*, that bird's up to his beak in all this murky business.'

'How could he be?' Mr Jones said. 'He was just crossing the road when the motorbike went by.'

'Maybe they slipped him the cash as they passed.'

'In that case we'd have seen it, wouldn't we? Do you know who the motorbike belongs to?'

'It was found abandoned on the Rumberloo Line embankment, where it comes out of the tunnel. We've a theory, but I'm not telling *you*; your family's under suspicion. Don't leave the district without informing us.'

Mr Jones said he had no intention of leaving. 'We want Mortimer found. My daughter's very upset.'

Arabel was more than upset, she was in despair. She wandered about the house all day, looking at the things that reminded her of Mortimer – the fireplace bricks without any mortar, the tattered hearthrug, the plates with beak-sized chips missing, the chewed upholstery, all the articles that turned up under carpets and lino, and the missing stairs. The carpenter hadn't come yet to replace them, and Mr Jones was too dejected to nag him.

'I wouldn't have thought I'd get fond of a bird so quick,' he said. 'I miss his sulky face, and his thoughtful ways, and the sound of him crunching about the house. Eat up your tea, Arabel, dearie,

there's a good girl. I expect Mortimer will find his way home by and by.'

But Arabel couldn't eat. Tears ran down her nose and on to her bread and jam until it was all soggy. That reminded her of the flood that Mortimer had caused by blocking up the bath plug, and the tears rolled even faster. 'Mortimer doesn't know our address!' she said. 'He doesn't even know our name!'

'We'll offer a five-pound reward for his return,' Mr Jones said.

'Five pounds!' cried Mrs Jones who had just come home from the supermarket where she now worked. 'Five pounds you offer for the return of that Fiend when already we owe eight hundred and seventeen pounds, and sixty-seven new pence to Round & Round, let alone the forty thousand to Peter Stone? The only thing that makes me thankful is that bird doesn't have to come with me to the supermarket!'

Just the same Mr Jones stuck up his Reward sign in the sub-post-office, alongside one from Peter Stone offering a thousand pounds for information that might lead to the return of his brooch, and similar ones from the bank, ironmonger and fishmonger.

Meanwhile, what of Mortimer and the squirrel?

They had flown as far as the tube station. There, Sam, by kicking Mortimer in the ribs and punching the top of his head, had directed him to fly into the station entrance.

Rumbury Tube Station is very old. The two entrances have big round arches with sliding openwork iron gates, and the station is faced all over with shiny raw-meat-coloured tiles. A dark-blue enamel sign says:

London General Omnibus & Subterranean Railway Company. By appmnt to His Majesty King Edward VII.

For nearly fifty years there had been only one slow, creaking old lift to take people down to the trains. A sign on it said '*Not authorized to carry more than 12 passengers.*' People too impatient to wait for it had to walk down about a thousand spiral stairs. But lately the station had been modernized by the addition of a handsome pair of escalators, one up, one down, which replaced the spiral stairs. Nothing else was modern: the ticket machines were so old that people said they would work only for a Queen Victoria bun penny, the bookstall was always shut, and had copies of the *Morning Post* for August 4, 1914, covered in dust; and the chocolate machines had been empty for generations.

Down below, as well as the train platforms, there were all kinds of mysterious old galleries, for in the days when trams still ran in London it had also been an underground tramway station, connecting with the Kingsway, Aldwych, and Spurgeon's Tabernacle line.

Not many trains stop at Rumbury Town; most of them rush straight through from Nutmeg Hill to Canon's Green.

Old Mr Gumbrell, the booking clerk, was Mr Jones's uncle. Besides selling tickets he also ran the lift. He was too shortsighted to see across to the lift from the ticket office, so when he had sold twelve tickets he would lock up his office and take the lift down. This meant that sometimes people had to wait a very long time but it didn't much matter, as there probably wouldn't be a train for hours anyway. However, in the end there were complaints, which was why the escalators were installed. Mr Gumbrell enjoyed riding on these, which he called escatailors; he used to leave the lift at the bottom and travel back up the moving stairs.

He did this today. He ran the lift slowly down, never noticing that Mortimer, with Sam the squirrel still grimly clutching him, was perched high up near the ceiling on the frame of a poster advertising the Pickwick, the Owl and the Waverly Pen.

Mr Gumbrell left the lift at the bottom, and sailed back up the escalator, mumbling to himself: 'Arr, these-ere moving stairs do be an amazing wonder of science. Whatever will they think of next?'

When Mr Gumbrell got to the top again he found the police there, examining the trail of cheese-crumbs which stopped outside the station entrance. They stayed a long time, but Mr Gumbrell could give them no useful information.

'Birds and squirrels!' he muttered when they had gone. 'Is it likely you'd be a-seeing birds and squirrels with di'mond brooches in a tube station?'

The phone rang. There was only one telephone in the station, a public phone booth with the door missing, so if people wanted to ring up Mr Gumbrell – which did not often happen – they rang on that line.

This time it was Mr Jones.

'Is that you, Uncle Arthur?'

'O' course it's me. Who else would it be?'

'We just wondered if you'd seen Arabel's raven. The trail of cheese crumbs led up your way, the police said.'

'No, I have not seen a raven,' snapped Mr Gumbrell. 'Coppers a-bothering here all afternoon, but still I haven't! Nor I haven't seen a Socrates bird nor a cassodactyl nor a pterowary. This is a tube station, not a zoological garden.'

'Will you keep a look-out, just the same?' said Mr Jones.

Mr Gumbrell thumped back the receiver. He was fed up with all the bother.

'Do I wait here any longer,' he said to himself, 'likely the militia and the beef-guards and the horse-eaters and the traffic wardens'll be along too. I'm closing up.'

Rumbury Town Station was not supposed to be closed except between 1 A.M. and 5 A.M., but in fact old Mr Gumbrell often did close it earlier if his bad toe was bothering him. No one had complained yet.

'Even if me toe ain't aching now, likely it'll start any minute, with all this willocking about,' Mr Gumbrell argued to himself. So he switched off the escalators, locked the lift gates and ticket office, turned out the lights, rang up Nutmeg Hill and Canon's Green to tell them not to let any trains stop, padlocked the big main mesh gates, and stomped off home to supper.

Next morning there were several people waiting to catch the first train to work when Mr Gumbrell arrived to open up. They bustled in as soon as he slid the gates back and didn't stop at the booking office for they all had season tickets. But when they reached the top of the escalator they did stop, in dismay and astonishment.

For the escalators were not there: nothing but a big gaping black hole.

'Someone's pinched the stairs,' said a Covent Garden porter.

'Don't be so soft. How could you pinch an escalator?' said a milkman.

'Well, they're gone, aren't they?' said a bus driver. 'What's *your* theory? Earthquake? Sunk into the ground?'

'Squatters,' said a train driver. 'Mark my words, squatters have taken 'em.'

'How'd they get through the locked gates? Anyway, what'd they take them *for*?'

'To squat on, of course.'

Mr Gumbrell stood scratching his head. 'Took my escatailors,' he said sorrowfully. 'What did they want to go and do that for? If they'd 'a took

the lift, now, I wouldn't 'a minded near as much. Well, all you lot'll have to go down in the lift, anyways – there ain't twelve of ye, so it's all right.'

It wasn't all right, though. When he pulled the lever that ought to have brought the lift up, nothing happened.

'And I'll tell you why,' said the train driver, peering through the closed top gates. 'Someone's been and chawed through the lift cable.'

'Sawed through it?'

'No, kind of chewed or haggled through; a right messy job. Lucky the current was switched off, or whoever done it would have been frizzled like popcorn.'

'Someone's been sabotaging the station,' said the bus driver. 'Football fans, is my guess.'

'Hippies, more like.'

'Someone ought to tell the cops.'

'Cops!' grumbled Mr Gumbrell. 'Not likely! Had enough of them in yesterday a-scavenging about for ravens and squirrels.'

Another reason why he did not want the police called in was because he didn't want to admit that he had left the station unattended for so long. But the early travellers, finding they could not get a train there, walked off to the next stop down the line, Nutmeg Hill. They told their friends at work what had happened, and the story spread. Presently a reporter from the *Rumbury Borough News* rang up the tube station for confirmation of the tale.

'Is that Rumbury Town Station? Can you tell me, please, if the trains are running normally?'

'Nevermore!' croaked a harsh voice, and the receiver was thumped down.

'You'd better go up there and have a look around,' said the *Borough News* editor, when his reporter told him of this puzzling conversation.

So the reporter – his name was Dick Otter – took a bus up to the tube station.

It was a dark, drizzly foggy day, and when he peered in through the station entrance he thought that it looked like a cave inside, under the round arches – the ticket machines, with their dim little lights, were like stalagmites, the white tiled floor was like a sheet of ice, the empty green chocolate machines were like hanks of moss dangling against the walls, and old Mr Gumbrell, with his white whiskers, seated inside the ticket booth, was like some wizened goblin with his little piles of magic cards telling people where they could go.

'Is the station open?' Dick asked.

'*You* walked in, didn't you? But you can't *go* anywhere,' said Mr Gumbrell.

Dick went over and looked at the gaping hole where the escalators used to be. Mr Gumbrell had hung a couple of chains across, to stop people from falling down.

Then Dick peered through the lift gates and down the shaft.

Then he went back to Mr Gumbrell, who was reading yesterday's football results by the light of a candle. It was very dark in the station entrance because nearly all the light switches were down below and Mr Gumbrell could not get at them.

'Who do you think took the escalators?' Dick asked, getting out his notebook.

Mr Gumbrell had been thinking about this a good deal, on and off, during the morning.

'Spooks,' he replied. 'Spooks what doesn't like modern inventions. I reckon the station's haunted. As I've bin sitting here this morning, there's a ghostly voice what sometimes comes and croaks in me lughole. "Nevermore," it says, "nevermore." That's one reason why I haven't informed the cops. What could they do? What that voice means is that this station shall nevermore be used.'

'I see,' said Dick thoughtfully. In his notebook he wrote 'Is Tube Station Haunted or Is Ticket Clerk Round the Bend?'

'What else makes you think it's haunted?' he asked.

'Well,' said Mr Gumbrell, 'there couldn't *be* anybody downstairs, could there? I locked up last night, when the nine o'clock south had gone, and I phoned 'em at Nutmeg Hill and Canon's Green not to let any trains stop here till I give 'em the word again. No one would 'a gone down this end after that, and yet sometimes I thinks as I can hear voices down the lift shaft a-calling out '*Help, help.*' Which is a contradiction of nature, since, like I said, no one could be down there.'

'Supposing they'd gone down last night before you locked up?'

'Then they'd 'a caught the nine o'clock south, wouldn't they? No, 'tis ghosties down there all right.'

'Whose ghosts, do you think?'

''Tis the ghosties of they old tram-car drivers. Why do I think that? Well, you look at these 'ere tickets.'

Mr Gumbrell showed a pile of green tenpenny tube tickets. Each had a large triangular snip taken from one side.

'See! A ghostie did that!' he said triumphantly. 'Who else could 'a got into my ticket office? The only way in was through the slot, see, where the passengers pays their fares. A 'yuman couldn't get through there, but a ghostie could. It was the ghostie of one of they old tram-car conductors, a-hankering to clip a ticket again like in bygone days, see? And the same ghostie pinched the ham sandwich I'd been a-saving for me breakfast and left nowt but crumbs. That's why I haven't rung Head Office, neether, cos what would be the use? If they did put in a pair of new escatailors and fix the lift, the new ones'd be gone again by next day. That's what the voice means when it says, "Nevermore."'

'You think you can hear voices crying "help, help" down the lift shaft?'

Dick went and listened but there was nothing to be heard at that moment.

'Likely I'm the only man as can hear 'em,' said Mr Gumbrell.

'It seems to me I can *smell* something though,' Dick said, sniffing.

Up from the lift shaft floated the usual smell of tube station – a strange, warm, dusty, metallic smell like powdered ginger. But as well as that there was another smell – fragrant and tantalizing.

'Smells to me like coffee,' Dick said.

'There you are, then!' cried Mr Gumbrell triumphantly. 'They old tram-car drivers used to brew up a big pot o' coffee when they was waiting for the last tram back to Brixton of a night-time.'

'I'd like to get some pictures of the station,' said Dick, and he went over to the public call-box and dialled his office, to get a photographer. But as he waited with the coin in his hand, ready to put it in the slot when the pips went, something large and black suddenly wafted past his head in the gloom, snatched the receiver from him, and whispered harshly in his ear,

'Nevermore!'

Next day the *Rumbury Borough News* had headlines:

'IS OUR TUBE STATION HAUNTED? Mr Gumbrell, ticket collector and clerk there for the last forty years, asserts that it is. 'Ghosts of old-time tram-car drivers sit downstairs,' he says, "playing dominoes and drinking licorice water." ' (Dick Otter had phoned his story from the call-box in the sub-post-office and the girl in the newsroom had misheard 'drinking coffee' as 'drinking toffee' which she rightly thought was nonsense, so she changed it to 'drinking licorice water'.)

'Shan't be able to meet people's eyes in the street,' said Mr Jones at breakfast. 'Going barmy, Uncle Arthur is, without a doubt. Haunted police station? Take him along to see the doctor, shall I?'

The postman rang, with a Recorded Delivery letter from a firm of lawyers: Messrs. Gumme, Harbottle, Inkpen and Rule. It said:

Dear Madam, acting as solicitors for Mr Round and Mr Toby Round, we wish to know when it will be convenient for you to pay the eight hundred and seventeen pounds, sixty-seven new pence' worth of damages that you owe our clients for Destruction of Premises?

This threw Mrs Jones into a dreadful flutter.

'That I should live to see the day when we are turned out of house and home on account of some fiend of a bird fetched in off the street by my own husband and dragged about on a red wooden truck by my own daughter!'

'Well, you haven't lived to see the day yet,' said Mr Jones. 'Wild creatures, ravens are counted as, in law, so we can't be held responsible for the bird's actions. I'll go around and tell them so, and *you*'d better do something to cheer up Arabel. I've never seen the child so thin and mopey.'

He drove his taxi up to Round & Round, the record shop, but, strangely enough, neither Mr Round nor Mr Toby Round was to be seen; the place was locked, silent and dusty.

After trying to persuade Arabel to eat her breakfast – which was no use, as Arabel wouldn't touch it – Mrs Jones decided to ring Uncle Arthur and tell him he should see a doctor for his nerves. She called up the tube station, but the telephone rang and rang and nobody answered. (In fact, the reason for this was that a great many sightseers, having read the piece in the *Borough News*, had come to stare at the station, and Mr Gumbrell was having a fine time telling them all about the ways of the old tram-car drivers.) While Mrs Jones was still holding the telephone and listening to the bell ring, another bell rang, louder: the front door bell.

'Trouble, trouble, nothing but trouble,' grumbled Mrs Jones. 'Here, Arabel, lovey, hold the phone and say 'Hallo, Uncle Arthur, Mum wants to speak to you,' if he answers, will you, while I see who's at the front door.'

Arabel took the receiver and Mrs Jones went to the front door where there were two policemen. She let out a screech.

'It's no use that pair of sharks sending you to arrest me for their eight hundred and seventeen pounds – I haven't got it if you were to turn me upside down and shake me till September!'

The police looked puzzled and one of them said, 'I reckon there's some mistake. We don't want to turn you upside down – we came to ask if you recognize this?'

He held out a small object in the palm of his hand.

Mrs Jones had a close look at it.

'Why certainly I do,' she said. 'That's Mr Round's tiepin – the one he had made out of one of his back teeth when it fell out as he ate a plateful of Irish stew.'

Meanwhile, Arabel was still sitting on the stairs holding the phone to her ear, when all at once she heard a hoarse whisper:

'Nevermore!'

Arabel was so astonished she almost dropped the telephone. She looked all around her – nobody there. Then she looked back at the phone, but it

had gone silent again. After a minute a different
voice barked,

'Who's that?'

'Hullo, Uncle Arthur, it's me, Arabel. Ma wants
to speak to you.'

'Well, I don't want to speak to her,' said
Mr Gumbrell, and he hung up.

Arabel sat on the stairs and she said to herself,

'That was Mortimer and he must be up at the
tube station because that's where Uncle Arthur is.'

Arabel had often travelled by tube and knew the
way to the station. She got her red truck, and she

put on her thick warm woolly coat, and she went out the back door because her mother was still talking at the front and Arabel didn't want to be stopped. She walked up the High Street, past the bank. The manager looked out and said to himself,

'That child's too young to be out on her own, I'd better follow her and find who she belongs to.'

He started after her.

Next Arabel passed the supermarket. The manager looked out and said to himself,

'That's Mrs Jones's little girl. I'll just nip after her and ask her where her mother's got to today.' So he followed Arabel.

Then she passed the Round & Round record shop, but there was nobody in it, and Mr Jones had become tired of waiting and driven off in his taxi.

Then she passed Peter Stone, the jeweller's. Peter Stone saw her through the window and thought, 'That girl looks as if she knows where she means to go. And she was the only one who showed any sense after my burglary. Maybe it was a true story about the squirrel and the raven. Anyway, no harm following her, to see where she goes.' So he locked up his shop and followed.

Arabel passed the fire station. Usually the firemen waved to her – they had been friendly ever since they'd had to come and climb in the Joneses' bathroom window – but today they were all hastily pulling on their helmets and rushing about. And just as she had gone past, the fire engine shot out into the street and went by going lickety-split.

Presently Arabel came to the tube station. The first person she saw there was her great-aunt Annie Gumbrell.

'*Arabel Jones!* What are you doing walking up the High Street by yourself, liable to get run over and kidnapped and murdered and abducted and worse? The idea! Where's your mother? And where are you going?'

'I'm looking for Mortimer,' said Arabel, and she kept on going. 'I've stayed on the same side all the way; I didn't have to cross over,' she said over her shoulder as she went into the tube station.

Aunt Annie had come up to the station to tell Uncle Arthur that he was behaving foolishly and had better come home, but she couldn't get near him because of the crowd. In fact, Arabel was the only person who *could* get into the station entrance now, because she was so small – there was just room for her and then the place was completely crammed. Aunt Annie wasn't able to get in at all. When Arabel was inside somebody kindly picked her up and set her on top of a ticket machine so that she could see.

'What's happening?' she asked.

'They reckon someone's stuck in the lift, down at the bottom. So they're a-going to send down a fireman, and he'll go in through the trap door in the roof of the lift and fetch 'em back,' said her great-uncle Arthur, who happened to be standing by her. 'I've told 'em and told 'em 'tis the ghosties of old tram drivers, but they don't take no notice.'

'Why don't they just send a train from Nutmeg Hill so someone can see what the matter is?'

'Train drivers' union won't let 'em stop. They say if 'tis the ghosties of old tram drivers stuck in the lift, 'tis a different union and no concern of theirn.'

Now the firemen, who had been taking a careful look at the lift, asked everybody to please step out into the street to make room. Then they rigged up a light, because the station was so dark, and they brought in a hoist, which was mostly used for rescuing people who got stuck on church spires or the roofs of burning buildings. So they let down a fireman in a sling, and the whole population of Rumbury Town, by now standing in the street outside, said,

'Coo!' and held their breath.

Presently a shout came from below.

'They've found someone,' said the firemen, and everybody said, 'Coo!' again and held their breath some more.

Just at this moment Arabel (still sitting on the fivepenny ticket machine for she was in no one's way there) felt a thump on her right shoulder. It was lucky that she had put on her thick warm woolly coat, for two claws took hold of her shoulder with a grip like a bulldog clip, and a loving croak in her ear said,

'*Nevermore!*'

'Mortimer!' cried Arabel, and she was so pleased that she might have toppled off the ticket machine if Mortimer hadn't spread out his wings like a tightrope-walker's umbrella and balanced them both.

Mortimer was just as pleased to see Arabel as she was to see him. When he had them both balanced he wrapped his left-hand wing round her and said, 'Nevermore' five or six times over, in tones of great satisfaction and enthusiasm.

'Look, Mortimer, they're bringing someone up.'

Who should climb out but Mr Toby Round, looking hungry and sorry for himself. The minute he was landed all sorts of helpful people, St John Ambulance men and stretcher-bearers and clergymen and the matron of the Rumbury

Hospital, all rushed at him with bandages and cups of tea and said, 'Are you all right?'

They would have taken him away, but he said he wanted to wait for his brother.

The sling went down again at once. In a few minutes up it came with the other Mr Round. As soon as he landed he noticed Arabel and Mortimer, perched on the ticket machine, and the sight of them seemed to set him in a passion.

'Grab that bird!' he shouted. '*He*'s the cause of all the trouble! Gnawed through the lift cable and ate the escalator and had my brother and me trapped in utter discomfort for forty-eight hours!'

'And what was you a-doing down there,' said Mr Gumbrell suspiciously, 'after the nine o'clock south had come and gone?'

Just at this moment a whole van load of police arrived with Mrs Jones, who seemed half distracted.

'*There* you are!' she screamed when she saw Arabel. 'And me nearly frantic. *Oh*, my goodness,

there's that great awful bird, as if we hadn't enough to worry us!'

But the police swarmed about the Round brothers, and the sergeant said, 'I have a warrant to arrest you two on suspicion of having pinched the cash from the bank last month and if you want to know why we think it's you that did it, it's because we found your tooth tie-pin left behind in the safe and one of Toby's fingerprints on the abandoned motorbike, and I shouldn't wonder if you did the jobs at the supermarket and the jeweller's and all the others too.'

'It's not true!' shouted Mr Toby Round. 'We didn't do it! We didn't do *any* of them. We were staying with my sister-in-law at Romford on each occasion. Her name's Mrs Flossie Wilkes and she lives at two-nought-nought-one Station Approach. If you ask *my* opinion that raven is the thief –'

But the sergeant had pulled Mr Toby Round's hand from his pocket to put a handcuff on it, and when he did so, what should come out as well but Sam the squirrel, and what should Sam be clutching in his paws but Mr Peter Stone's diamond brooch worth forty thousand pounds.

So everybody said, 'Coo,' again.

And Mr Round and Mr Toby Round were taken off to Rumbury Hill Police Station.

The police sergeant hitched a ride in the firemen's sling and went down the lift shaft and had a look around the old galleries and disused tram station, and he found the money that had been stolen from the bank, all packed in the plastic dustbins that had been stolen from Brown's the ironmonger's and he found nine hundred and ninety-nine of the thousand tins of Best Jamaica blend coffee stolen from the supermarket, and a whole lot of other things that must have been stolen from different premises all over Rumbury Town.

While he was making these exciting discoveries down below, up above, Mrs Jones was saying,

'Arabel, you come home directly, and don't you dare go out on your own ever again!'

'Nevermore!' said Mortimer.

So Arabel climbed down from the ticket machine with Mortimer still on her shoulder.

'Here!' said Uncle Arthur, who had been silent for a long time, turning things over in his mind, 'that bird ought to be arrested too, if he's the one what ate my escatailors and put my lift out of order, and how do we know he wasn't in with those blokes with their burglaries? He was the one what helped the squirrel make off with the di'mond brooch.'

'He was flyjacked; he couldn't help it,' said Arabel.

'Far from being arrested,' said the bank manager, 'he'll get a reward from the bank for helping to bring the criminals to justice.'

'And he'll get one from me too,' said Peter Stone.

'And from me,' said the supermarket manager.

'Come along, Arabel, do,' said Mrs Jones. 'Oh my gracious, look at the time, your father'll be home wanting his tea and wondering where in the world we've got to.'

Arabel collected her red truck, which she had left outside, and Mortimer climbed on to it.

'My stars!' cried Mrs Jones. 'You're not going to pull that great black sulky bird all the way home on the truck when we know perfectly *well* he can fly, the lazy thing? Never did I hear anything so outrageous, never!'

'He likes being pulled,' said Arabel, so that was the way they went home. The bank manager and the supermarket manager and Mr Peter Stone and quite a lot of other people saw them as far as their gate.

Mr Jones was inside and had just made a pot of tea. When he saw them come in the front gate he poured out an eggcupful for Mortimer.

They all sat round the kitchen table and had tea. Mortimer had several egg-cupfuls, and as for Arabel, she made up for all the meals she had missed while Mortimer had been lost.

The Escaped Black Mamba

IT WAS NOT long after Mortimer the raven took up residence with the Jones family, at Number Six, Rainwater Crescent, Rumbury Town, London, NW 3½, that Mr and Mrs Jones received an invitation to the Furriers' Freewheeling Ball, at the Assembly Rooms, Rumbury Town.

'What is a Freewheeling Ball?' asked Arabel.

She was eating her breakfast. Mortimer the raven was sitting on her shoulder and peering down into her boiled egg to see if there were any diamonds in it. Mortimer was going through a phase of hoping to find diamonds everywhere.

There were no diamonds in the egg.

'A Freewheeling Ball,' said Mr Jones, gloomily putting on his taxi-driving overcoat, 'is six hours on your feet after a long hard day's work, with your best suit throttling you, and nothing to eat but potato crisps.'

'Kaark,' said Mortimer. He loved potato crisps almost as much as diamonds.

Arabel imagined them all in their best clothes, pushing a huge freewheeling ball round and round the Assembly Rooms, which were very grand, with red walls and bunches of gold grapes dangling down them.

'You will go to the ball, won't you?' she said anxiously. 'Then Chris Cross can come to babysit.'

'I daresay we'll have to,' said Mr Jones, looking at the hopeful faces of his wife and daughter. 'But mind! If Chris comes he's not to play his guitar after eleven at night. Last time we had trouble from the neighbours right up to the High Street.'

He kissed his family goodbye, nodded to Mortimer and went off to drive his taxi.

As he shut the front door Mortimer fell head first into Arabel's boiled egg.

'Oh my good gracious, Arabel,' said Mrs Jones, 'why in the name of mystery you can't teach that dratted bird to *balance* I don't know. You'd think a creature with wings would have the sense not to lean forward till he topples over. *Look* at the mess! If I lived to ninety and ended my days

in Pernambuco I doubt if I'd see anything to
equal it!'

'Nevermore,' said Mortimer. As his head was
still inside the boiled egg, the word came out
muffled.

'Do they have boiled eggs in Pernambuco?' said
Arabel.

'How should I know?' said Mrs Jones crossly,
clearing away the breakfast things. 'For gracious'
sake, Arabel, put that bird in the bath and run the
tap on him. How I shall ever get to the office in
time I can't imagine.'

Mrs Jones now worked at Nuggett & Coke, the
coal order office. Arabel and Mortimer loved
calling in to see her there; Arabel loved the
beautiful blazing fire that always burned in a
shiny red stove, and Mortimer liked the sample
lumps of coal in pink bowls on the counter.

Arabel didn't put Mortimer in the bath. She put
him, boiled egg and all, on to her red truck and
pulled him into the garden. Mortimer never
walked if he could ride. And he never flew at all.

'That bird's got an egg on his head,' said the
milkman, leaving two bottles of Jersey, two of
orange, a dairy cake, a dozen ham-flavoured eggs
and three yoghurts (one rum, one brandy, one
Worcestershire sauce).

'Why shouldn't he, if he wants to?' said Arabel. The milkman had no answer to this, so he went on, jangling up the street in his electric trolley.

Presently the egg fell off, Granny came along to look after Arabel and Mortimer, and Mrs Jones went off to to work.

Granny made pancakes for lunch and Mortimer helped toss. Granny did not entirely approve of this, but Arabel said probably there were no pancakes where Mortimer came from and he should have a chance to learn what they were like.

Anyway, they got the kitchen floor scrubbed long before Mrs Jones came home.

On the night of the Furriers' Freewheeling Ball Chris Cross came in to babysit.

Arabel loved Chris. He was not very old, still doing his A-levels at Rumbury Comprehensive, and he had first-rate ideas about how to pass the evening when he came to the Joneses. He thought of something different and new each time. Last time they had made a Midsummer Pudding, using everything in the kitchen. Also he sang and played beautiful tunes on his guitar.

'Arabel's to go to bed at half-past eight,' said Mr Jones.

'What about Mortimer?' said Chris. He and Mortimer had not met before; they took a careful look at one another.

'He goes when he likes. But he is *not* to sleep in the fridge *or* in the airing cupboard,' said Mrs Jones, putting on her coat. She was wearing a pink satin dress with beads on it.

'Not too noisy on that guitar, now,' said Mr Jones.

'I brought my trumpet too; I'll play that instead if you like,' said Chris.

Mr Jones said the guitar would be better.

'And no trumpet after eight, *definitely*,' he said.

'Supper's in the kitchen,' said Mrs Jones. 'Mince pies and cheese patties and tomatoes and crisps.'

'Kaark,' said Mortimer.

'What flavour crisps?' said Arabel.

'Sardine.'

Mr and Mrs Jones went off in his taxi and Chris at once began singing a lullaby.

*'Morning moon, trespassing down over my
    skylight's shoulder,
Who asked you in, to doodle across my
    deep-seated dream?*

*– Basso bluebells chiming to ice as the night
grows colder –*
*Be off! Toboggan away on your bothering
beam!'*

Arabel loved listening to Chris sing. She stuck her finger in her mouth and sat quite still. Mortimer perched in the coal scuttle, listening too. He had never heard anybody play the guitar before. He began to get over-excited; he jumped up and down in the coal scuttle about a hundred times, opening and shutting his wings and shouting, 'Nevermore!'

'Doesn't he like the song?' said Chris.

'Oh yes, he *does*,' said Arabel. 'It's just that he's not used to it.'

'Maybe we'd better dress up as Vikings and play hide-and-seek.'

'How do we dress as Vikings?'

'In cloaks and helmets.'

Arabel used a saucepan as a helmet and Chris used the pressure cooker.

'A towel's going to be too big for Mortimer,' she said.

'He can have a face-towel. And a sardine tin as a helmet.'

Arabel thought a frozen orange-juice tin would be a better shape.

Mortimer was very amazed at his Viking costume. They fastened his face-towel on with safety-pins. When it was his turn to hide he climbed into the airing cupboard (they had opened it to get out the towels). While he was in the cupboard he had a good hunt for diamonds, tearing some sheets and pillow-cases and leaving coaly footprints on Mrs Jones's terylene lawn nightdress. He did not discover any diamonds. His helmet fell off.

'The cupboard is terribly hot,' said Arabel, when she found Mortimer. (She had guessed where to look right away, as he was so fond of the airing cupboard.) 'My goodness, Ma went out leaving the immersion heater switched on, the hot-water tank is almost boiling. I had better switch it off.' She did so.

'Ma will be pleased that I thought of doing that,' she said.

When it was Chris's turn to hide, it took a very long time to find him, as he had packed himself tightly into the laundry basket and pulled the lid down over his head. He had a book in his pocket, for he had intended to read, but went to sleep instead.

Arabel hunted for Chris all over the house.

Mortimer, meanwhile, had another idea. He was wondering if there might be any diamonds in the hole inside Chris's guitar. He went off to have a look, leaving Arabel to hunt by herself. She found her right gumboot, which had been missing for a week, she found a chocolate egg left over from last Easter, she found three pancakes that Mortimer had hidden inside the record player and forgotten, but she did not find Chris.

However, Mortimer was annoyed to discover that Chris, who never took chances with his beautiful guitar, had placed it and the trumpet on top of the broom cupboard. Since Mortimer never flew if he could possibly avoid it, the guitar was out of his reach.

He looked angrily around the kitchen with his bright eyes that were as black as privet-berries.

The ironing board stood not far away.

Mortimer was very strong. He began shoving the ironing board across the kitchen floor. After five minutes he had it up against the cupboard.

Meanwhile, Arabel was still hunting for Chris. She looked in the hat and coat cupboard under the stairs. There she found a plastic spade left over from Littlehampton last summer, and two bottles of champagne, which Mr Jones had hidden there as a Christmas surprise for Mrs Jones. No Chris.

Mortimer, in the meantime, was considering, looking at the ironing board. Then he knocked over the waste bucket, tipping out the waste, got on to a chair, holding the bucket in one claw, and climbed from the chair on to the ironing board. He put the bucket on the ironing board, upside down, and got on top of it.

He still could not quite reach the top of the broom cupboard.

Arabel looked for Chris under all the beds. She did not find him, but she found one of her blue bedsocks, a ginger biscuit, last Sunday's colour supplement, and a tooth she had lost three weeks before.

Mortimer got down from the waste bucket and found a square cheese grater. He made his way back on to the ironing board, reached up and balanced the cheese grater on top of the upside-down bucket;

then he clambered carefully up and stood tip-claw on the cheese-grater's rim.

Still he could not quite reach the top of the broom cupboard.

Arabel looked for Chris under the bath. She did not find him, but she found all the pearl-handled knives and forks, Mrs Jones's wedding-present fruit set that had disappeared shortly after Mortimer came to live in the house. It had been thought that a burglar had taken them.

'Ma *will* be pleased,' Arabel said. She carried all the knives and forks to the kitchen in a fold of her Viking towel.

When she reached the kitchen the first thing she saw was Mortimer.

He had jammed a milk bottle into the cheese grater, which was on top of the bucket, which was upside down on the ironing board, and he was now carefully climbing up so as to stand on top of the milk bottle.

'Oh, Mortimer,' said Arabel.

At the sound of her voice Mortimer turned his head.

A lot of things happened at once. The bucket fell off the ironing board, which fell over, the cheese grater fell off the bucket, the milk bottle

(full of best Jersey milk) fell out of the cheese grater with Mortimer clinging on to it.

The noise, a loud, grinding, scrunching clatter like the sound of a dustbin lorry, woke Chris, curled up asleep inside the laundry basket. He came to see what was happening in the kitchen.

Arabel had a brush and dustpan and she was sweeping up bits of broken glass. Mortimer was sitting on the fender looking ruffled. There were splashes of best Jersey milk all over the floor and some large puddles. Quite a few other things were on the floor too.

'It's a good thing we had two bottles of milk,' Arabel said, remembering that Chris was very fond of milk.

'What happened?' said Chris, yawning.

'I think Mortimer wanted to look at your guitar.'

'Nevermore,' said Mortimer, but he didn't sound as if he meant it.

'It had better stay on top of the cupboard for now,' said Chris, giving Mortimer a hard look.

'Shall we have supper, as we're all in the kitchen?' said Arabel.

So they had supper and Mortimer cheered up.

He was not keen on the cheese patties Mrs Jones had made, so Arabel got some frozen braised beef (which he was *very* keen on) out of the fridge.

While she was thawing it under the hot tap Mortimer sat on the cold tap, jumping up and down with impatience and muttering, 'Nevermore,' under his breath. When he was too excited to wait any longer he took the packet from her, whacked a hole in the foil with his big, sharp, hairy beak, and ate the braised beef in a very messy way. Arabel spread the evening paper on the floor, and some of the gravy went on that.

Then Mortimer realized, from the scrunching, that the others were eating crisps.

He climbed on to the arm of Arabel's chair.

'Do you want some crisps, Mortimer?'

Mortimer jumped up and down. His black eyes shone like the currants on sticky buns.

Arabel put a handful of crisps on the table in front of him.

Mortimer began eating them as he had the pancakes; he tossed each one in the air and then tried to spear it with his beak before it fell.

All things considered, he was remarkably good at this; much better than Chris and Arabel, who began trying to do it too. But they hadn't got beaks, and had to catch the crisps in their mouths.

Mortimer was spearing his forty-ninth crisp when he hit the milk bottle which was standing on the table beside Chris. It fell to the floor and broke.

'It's lucky we'd drunk half the milk already,' said Arabel.

Unfortunately, Chris cut his hand while picking up bits of glass.

'Ma says you should always sweep up broken glass with a brush,' said Arabel. 'What's the matter, Chris?'

Chris had gone very quiet and white. Then he went green. He said, 'I always faint at the sight of blood.' Then he fainted, bumping against the broom cupboard as he went down. His trumpet was dislodged and fell to the floor.

'Oh dear, Mortimer,' Arabel said. 'It was a pity you knocked over that bottle. I wonder what we had better do now?'

Mortimer paid no attention. He was studying Chris's trumpet very attentively indeed; first he poked his beak into all the holes.

Arabel tried soaking a face-towel in the spilled milk and rubbing it on Chris's forehead. Then she switched on the fan heater to warm his bare feet. Then she put a spoonful of ginger marmalade into his mouth. That made him blink. Mortimer shouted, 'Nevermore!' in his ear. He blinked again and sat up.

'What happened?' he said.

'You fainted,' said Arabel.

'I always faint at the sight of blood.' He looked down at his cut finger.

'Well, don't faint again,' said Arabel. 'Here, put this round it.' She tore a strip from the face towel and bandaged Chris's finger with it.

He stood up, swaying a little.

'You ought to have brandy to make you better,' said Arabel. 'But Pa keeps the brandy in his taxi, in case of lady passengers turning faint.'

'I'd rather have milk,' said Chris.

However, both bottles of milk were now broken.

'There's a milk machine by the dairy in the High Street,' Chris said. 'I'll go and get some more.'

'Ma said you were not to go out and leave me,' said Arabel. 'I'll come too.'

'It's your bedtime.'

'No, it isn't, not for five minutes by the kitchen clock. We'd better go right away.'

Arabel decided that she did not need a coat, and she was still wearing her Viking costume, which was a very thick orange towel, and her saucepan helmet. She took the front-door key from the nail on the dresser.

'Come on, then,' said Chris.

'I wonder if Mortimer had better come too? Ma doesn't like him left alone in the house.'

When they looked around for Mortimer, who had been very quiet for a few minutes, they found that he had got himself jammed inside Chris's trumpet, face towel and all. They pulled at his feet, which stuck out, but they could not shift him.

'He must have been looking for diamonds,' said Arabel. 'We had better not wait. We can get him out when we come back; I expect if we trickle in a little cooking oil it will loosen him.'

'Thanks!' said Chris. 'Am I supposed to play my trumpet when it's full of sunflower oil?'

'Well, it would be better than engine oil,' said Arabel, 'and you can't play it when it's full of Mortimer.'

Luckily, Chris's trumpet had a hole in it (he had bought it for fifty pence at a charity shop and stuck a plaster over the hole when he played), so Mortimer was not likely to suffocate. Arabel put him on her red truck, with his feet sticking out of the trumpet, and they walked up to the top of Rainwater Crescent, where it joins on to Rumbury High Street at the traffic lights.

It was a dark, windy night. Nobody was about, though they could hear music and voices coming from the youth club at the other end of the street.

When they reached the milk machine by the dairy Chris found that he had nothing but a fifty-pence piece. The machine would only take fives.

'We could get change at the youth club,' said Arabel. 'It would be silly to go back without any milk now we've come so far.'

They walked towards the youth club. There was an arcade leading up to it, with fruit machines on each side. Arabel had a penny of her own, so she put it in one of the fruit machines. Some little red balls lit up and rushed about and clanked and shot through holes and bounced on levers and all of a sudden a whole shower of pennies, and five, ten and fifty pence pieces shot out into the metal cup on the machine's front and a big sign lit up that said, 'You are the winner! You are the next best thing to a millionaire! Why not have another go?'

Mortimer was amazed. As it happened, he had been looking that way, through the hole in the trumpet, when all this happened.

'Now we don't need to change your fifty-pence piece, which is good,' said Arabel. 'We can go back to the milk machine.'

So they turned round. Several people had noticed Arabel winning all the money, because the machine made such a commotion. A couple of sinister-looking men looked at Mortimer. Nothing could be seen of him but his stomach, the tips of his wings and tail, and his two feet with their hairy ankle frills sticking out of the trumpet.

'Look there!' said one of the men. 'I bet that's him!'

'I reckon you're right! Barmy sort of disguise though,' said the other.

'Come on, let's get after them!'

The men got into a sports car, which was parked illegally on the double-yellow lines by the

arcade, and followed Chris and Arabel along the street.

Chris put a five pence piece in the slot of the milk-vending machine. Wheels whirred and levers went up and down inside; presently a carton of milk came thumping down into the space in the middle.

This time Mortimer had been watching very intently through his hole. When the carton of milk came into view he said 'Kaark!' several times and began to jump up and down in the red truck, trumpet and all.

'I think he'd like you to put in another one,' Arabel said.

This time when Chris put in the coin, for some reason, the machine went wild and shot out six cartons of milk.

'My goodness,' said Arabel. 'We haven't paid for all that. You ought to put in five more.'

'I don't know,' said Chris. 'It isn't our fault if the machine goes crazy.'

'We can easily afford to. We've got ten pounds, and forty-three pence. I've been counting.'

So Chris put in five more coins. Nothing happened. The milk machine was tired out.

While Chris and Arabel were piling the seven cartons of milk on the red truck beside Mortimer, one of the two men in the sports car (which was now parked a little way off) whispered to the other,

'Reckon that's him all right, Bill, don't you?'

The other man nodded.

'The boss is going to be pretty pleased about this, hey, Sid? We'll snatch him back further along, where it's quiet.'

'Guess they've got him in that trumpet for a disguise.'

'Loopy sort of disguise,' muttered Bill, letting off the handbrake and letting the car roll slowly along the street.

Arabel, Chris and Mortimer were now on their way home. But Mortimer did not want to go home just yet. He had never seen automatic machines before; he thought they were the most interesting things he had seen in all his life, and he wanted to know all about them.

As the red truck passed Gaskett and Dent, the big garage on the corner, Mortimer looked out through the hole in his trumpet and said, 'Kaaaark!' Sometimes when he spoke inside the trumpet he accidentally blew quite a loud note. It happened this time, and the sports car swerved sharply across the road.

'What does Mortimer want?' said Chris.

'I think he would like us to put a coin in that machine.'

'All-night paraffin? What would we want *paraffin* for?'

'We could use it instead of cooking oil for getting Mortimer out of the trumpet.'

'Oh, very well,' said Chris. He put in a tenpenny piece and got a carton of paraffin. Mortimer would have liked him to do it again, but Chris thought one lot of paraffin was enough.

'There's a bread machine at the baker's,' Arabel said.

'It *must* be past your bedtime by now.'

'Well, we don't *know* that,' Arabel pointed out, 'because we none of us have watches. Mortimer would like to get a loaf from the bread machine.'

But at the baker's they had a disappointment. The bread machine was out of order. A sign said so.

'Nevermore,' said Mortimer, inside the trumpet.

'Poor thing, he does sound a bit sorry for himself in there,' said Chris. 'Tell you what, as we've come so far, we might as well go up to the tube station. There's lots of machines up there.'

'Oh *yes*!' said Arabel.

Rumbury Tube Station had recently been modernized inside, after an 'accident' to its lift and escalators. A whole lot of new automatic machines had been installed in the station entrance. One sold hot milk, soup, hot chocolate, tea and coffee, black or white, with or without sugar. Another had apples, pears, or bananas. Another had sandwiches and meat pies. Another had paperback books. Another would polish your shoes. Another would take a photograph of you looking as if you had seen a ghost. Another would massage the soles of your feet. Another would say a cheering poem and hold your hand while it did so. Another would print your name and address on a little tin disc. Another would tell your weight and horoscope. Another would blow your nose on a clean tissue, if you stuck your nose into a slot and, as well as that, give you a Vitamin C tablet and two mentholated throat lozenges, all for two and a half pence.

There was also a useful machine which would give you change for all the others.

Arabel's Uncle Arthur was the booking clerk. 'Arr,' he used to say, 'there's that variety of machines at Rumbury Toob now, a man wouldn't need kith nor kin nor wife nor fambly; he could just pass his life in the station and they wondrous machines'd do all he needed. Even his wash he could get done next door at the Washeteria; all they don't do for you is sleep.'

Uncle Arthur never needed anyone to do *his* sleeping for him. He was asleep now, with his head pillowed on a pile of tenpenny tickets, snoring like a brontosaurus.

Mortimer looked around at all the automatic machines with their little glass windows and things for sale all bright behind them; his eyes sparkled through the hole in the trumpet like buttons on patent-leather boots.

'Where shall we start?' said Arabel.

Sid and Bill left their car parked illegally outside on a double yellow line and strolled up to the station entrance. They stood leaning against the wall, looking in.

'Bit public here,' said Bill. Sid nodded.

It was at this moment in the Rumbury Town Assembly Rooms, in the middle of the Furriers' Freewheeling Ball, that Mrs Jones suddenly left her partner (Mr Finney the fishmonger), rushed up to Mr Jones, who was gloomily eating crisps at the buffet, grabbed his lapel, and said, 'Ben! I've just remembered! I left the immersion heater on! Oh my stars, do you suppose the tank will burst and all our sheets and towels be ruined, and what about Arabel and Mortimer and that boy Chris, though I daresay he can take care of himself; do you suppose they'll be scalded? Oh my goodness gracious, what a fool I am, what shall we do?'

'It won't burst,' said Mr Jones, 'but it'll be costing us a packet. I'll phone up home and tell Chris to switch it off.'

'I'll come to the phone with you,' said Mrs Jones, 'and make sure Arabel's in bed and everything's all right.'

There was a wall telephone in the Assembly Rooms lobby. Mr Jones dialled his home number but nobody answered. The bell rang and rang.

'Funny,' he said. 'Maybe I got the wrong number. I'll try again.'

He tried again. Still no answer.

'Oh, Ben!' said Mrs Jones fearfully. 'What can have happened? Can the house have burned down?'

'Don't be silly, Martha. How could the phone ring if the house had burned down? Maybe it's a crossed line. I'll get the exchange to ring them.'

He got the exchange. But all they could say was that nobody was answering on Rumbury o-one-one-o.

'Oh, Ben! What can have happened? Do you think the boiler did burst? Or perhaps there's been a gas escape and they're all lying unconscious or masked gunmen are holding them up and they aren't allowed to phone or there was something deadly in those cheese patties and they're in agony trying to crawl down the stairs or maybe there's a black mamba escaped from the zoo coiled round the banisters and they can't get by. I've always *said* it

was silly to have the phone halfway up the stairs, oh my gracious, we must go home directly!'

'Don't be silly. We haven't *got* gas, Martha, so how could it escape?'

'From the zoo!' cried Mrs Jones, frantically waving her cloakroom ticket at the lady who was knitting by the counter. 'Oh, please, dear, find my coat quick, there's a love, for a deadly masked mamba has escaped from the gasworks and it's got into the cheese patties and if we don't get home directly there won't be one of them alive to tell the tale!'

'What tale?' said the cloakroom lady, rather puzzled, and she was even more puzzled when she looked at the ticket which said 'Clean and retexture one pink satin dress'.

'This one, this one, then,' said Mrs Jones, distractedly fishing out another ticket which said 'Rumbury Borough Library Non-fiction'. 'That one, that black coat with the sparkling butterfly brooch on the collar, oh please hurry, or I shall pass out with palpitations, I know I shall.'

'Why did Mr and Mrs Jones go off so quick?' asked the cloakroom lady's cousin, Mrs Finney, presently, bringing her some crisps and a glass of sparkling cideringo.

'Oh, Grace, it's awful! One of those deadly cheese mambas has escaped from the telephone exchange and there's gunmen going after it because its breath is like a poison gas and it's in Mr Jones's house coiled round the boiler and everybody's dead and someone just rang from the zoo to tell them to come home.'

'My lawks. I'd better tell my hubby, he's a great friend of poor Mr Jones. Perce, Perce, just listen to this: a deadly mamba has escaped from Mr Jones's house and it's in the telephone exchange with a gun and they're trying to gas it out with deadly cheese and all Mr Jones's family are unconscious inside the boiler and his house is burned down.'

'Cripes,' said Mr Finney, who was a member of the Auxiliary Fire Brigade. 'I'd best be off, they'll be wanting all the lads at that rate.' He went towards the entrance, muttering, 'I wonder why they got inside the boiler?'

'Take your gas mask!' his wife screeched after him.

Most of the men at the Furriers' Ball were glad of the excuse to stream after Mr Finney, and their wives followed, all agog to see what was happening at Number Six, Rainwater Crescent. A procession of cars started away from the Assembly Rooms, in pursuit of Mr Jones's taxi.

Meanwhile, Mr and Mrs Jones had arrived at Number Six.

'At least the *house* is still standing,' cried Mrs Jones. 'Open the door, Ben, do, I couldn't if I was to be turned to a nutmeg on the spot, my hand's all of a tremble and my saint pancreas is going round and round like a spin dryer.'

Mr Jones unlocked the door and they hurried in.

'Arabel,' called Mrs Jones. 'Arabel, dearie, where are you? It's Mum and Dad come home to save you!'

No answer.

Mrs Jones rushed to the kitchen, where the light was on, and screamed.

'Oh my dear cats alive! *Ben! Look!* Oh, whatever has been going on? Broken glass everywhere – blood – milk – towels – what's that guitar doing up on top of the cupboard? – cheese grater on the floor, crisps everywhere, pressure cooker in the laundry basket – a whole *gang* of mambas must have been in!'

Even Mr Jones was obliged to admit that it looked as if there had been a struggle.

'I'd best call the police,' he said unhappily, when he had been all over the house, and made sure that neither Arabel, Mortimer, nor Chris was anywhere in it. 'There's been something funny going on in the airing cupboard too; one thing, the intruders seem to have had the sense to turn off the immersion heater. Not before time, the water's boiling.'

'Oh, how can you talk about immersion heaters when my child's been gagged and tied up in a lot of sheets and towels,' lamented Mrs Jones. 'Kidnapped, that's what they've been, by a gang of those deadly gorillas that live in the River Jordan. Oh, Ben! We'll never set eyes on them again. My little Arabel! And Mortimer! To think I'll never see him digging for diamonds in the coal scuttle any more!'

'Oh, come, Martha, things may not be as bad as that,' said Mr Jones doubtfully. 'Let's see what the police say.' He went to the phone and dialled 999.

'Send back a lock of hair in a matchbox, they will,' wept Mrs Jones. 'Or a claw, maybe! Heart of gold that bird had at bottom; just a rough diamond with feathers on, he was. Many's the time I've seen him look at me as though he'd have *liked* to think a kind thought if his nature would have let him.'

'I want the police,' said Mr Jones into the telephone.

But at that moment the police came through the front door, which was open.

It was Sergeant Pike, who had met Mr Jones not long before when Mortimer helped to catch some bank robbers. With the sergeant there were two constables.

'Evening, Mr J,' said the sergeant. 'Someone up the town reported you've an escaped snake in the house, is that right?'

'Snake? Who said anything about a snake?' Mr Jones was puzzled. 'No, it's my daughter, and our raven Mortimer, and the babysitter who seem to have been overpowered and kidnapped, Sergeant. They aren't anywhere in the house. You can see there's been quite a fight here. Look at this blood on the floor.'

'Carried off to Swanee Arabia they've been by a band of gorillas,' sobbed Mrs Jones.

'That's yuman blood on the floor, that is,' said one of the constables, as if no one had noticed it before.

'You can see there's bin a struggle. Someone tore a strip off that towel.'

'For a gag, likely.'

'The guitar got tossed up on top of the cupboard in the roughhouse.'

'The ironing board got kicked over in the ruckus.'

'Someone bashed someone's head with a milk bottle.'

'And then the other bloke took and bashed him back with another bottle.'

'And collared him when he was down and scraped him with the cheese grater.'

'That'll be Grievous Bodily Harm, shouldn't wonder.'

'Cheese grater,' said the sergeant thoughtfully. 'Wasn't there something talked of in the town about poisoned cheese patties?'

Just at that moment there was a tremendous clanging of bells as the fire engine drew up outside.

'Can we help?' said Mr Finney who, with his mates, had jumped into their auxiliary fire uniforms and were eagerly brandishing their fire-axes.

'I dunno,' said the sergeant. 'Why are you all wearing gas masks?'

'Someone said a tank full of deadly mambas had exploded and there was gas about.'

Now all the ladies from the Furriers' Ball turned up looking like the chorus from a Greek play.

'We've brought hot tea and blankets,' cried Mrs Finney. 'Where's all the injured persons?'

'Strewth,' said the sergeant. 'How am I expected to get on, with all this shower?'

People swarmed over the house, looking at the mess. Every room was filled with ladies, blankets, firemen and axes.

'Do you find you can get your sink *really* clean with Dizz, dear?' said Mrs Finney to Mrs Jones. 'I find Swoosh ever so much better.'

'Fancy you still having those old-fashioned plastic curtains in your kitchen. Give it ever such an old-world look, don't they? *My* hubby *made* me change to blinds, ever so much more modern and Continental, he said.'

'Haven't you ever thought of getting a sink waste disposal unit, dear?'

'I have lost my beloved daughter and my greatly esteemed raven,' said Mrs Jones with dignity, 'and I should be obliged if you would leave me alone with my trouble.'

'Yes, why don't you ladies go and have a hunt up and down the street, see if you can lay eyes on the little girl,' said the sergeant, 'or one of these here pistol-packing mambas I hear talk of. Be off, clear out, that's right, let's have a bit of peace and quiet around here, can we?'

'Suppose we meet the mambas, what shall we do?'

'It isn't mambas, it's gorillas,' wailed Mrs Jones.

'Do not attempt to engage them in combat but inform the police,' said Sergeant Pike. 'If you patrol the High Street in half dozens I daresay you'll be safe enough.'

He shoved the reluctant ladies out of the house.

'What about us?' said Mr Finney, hopefully peering about for something to bash with his fireman's axe. In his gas mask he looked like some creature that has climbed up out of the deep, deep sea.

'You cruise up and down the High Street in your fire engine and assist the ladies in their enquiries,' instructed Sergeant Pike and shoved him out too. 'Now, Mr and Mrs Jones, if you'll just accompany me up to the station and make a statement, perhaps this case can proceed in a proper and orderly manner.'

'Why go up to the tube station? Oh my stars, why can't we make a statement here when all the time my Arabel's lying bound and gagged on some railway line in the desert with all the Arabian

Knights of the Round Table ready to chop her in half if she moves hand or foot?'

PC Smith and PC Brown, who had been searching the house, came to report.

'Someone's been incarcerated in the airing cupboard,' PC Smith said. 'There's an empty tin of orange juice there, also a ginger biscuit, a chocolate egg and three battered pancakes.'

'Ah,' said Sergeant Pike, 'that proves it was a carefully planned and premeditated job. The intruder must have been hiding in the airing cupboard before you left for the ball, Mr Jones, just waiting till you were out of the house.'

'He must have been ever so small, then,' wept Mrs Jones, 'for *I* never saw him when I turned the heater on for Arabel's bath. Oh my goodness, it must have been one of those wicked fiendish little dwarfs capable of superhuman strength like Mr Quilp in *The Old Curiosity Shop* or the hunchback of the Aswan Dam.'

'Let's get up to the station, for pete's sake,' said Sergeant Pike, who began to feel he was losing his grip on the case. 'Do you want to come in the police car or will you follow in your taxi?'

'We'll follow,' said Mr Jones. After the police had left he carefully locked the house, and he and Mrs Jones followed in the taxi. But they got left behind almost at once because whenever Mrs Jones laid eyes on a group of searching ladies she made her husband slow down while she put her head out of the window and shouted:

'It's not gorillas after all, it's those wicked little dwarf Arabian Knights with curved swords that go round cutting cushions in half in old curiosity shops.'

'Now, Mrs Jones,' said the superintendent, when they finally arrived at the police station, 'you say your daughter Arabel has been kidnapped?'

'*And* our raven Mortimer, and the babysitter, Chris Cross.'

'We'll take them one at a time, please. What was the babysitter doing when you last saw him?'

'He was playing his guitar and singing a song about a two-gun two-timing kid from Kansas.'

'That's very suspicious,' said the superintendent. 'Depend on it, the babysitter was in on the plot! And the raven?'

'He was throwing paper pellets out of the window.'

'Hmmm, he might have been sending messages to an accomplice?'

Mr Jones shook his head. 'Not Mortimer.'

'Why not?'

'No accomplice could stand Mortimer's ways.'

Meanwhile, up at Rumbury Tube Station, Arabel, Mortimer and Chris had been having a wonderful time. Mortimer, jumping up and down in frantic excitement inside his trumpet, had watched while they put coins into every single machine, one by one. On the red truck, as well as seven cartons of milk and the paraffin, they now had a packet of wine gums, two bars of chocolate, a packet of nuts and raisins, a ham sandwich, four empty cups (one chocolate, one milk, one coffee, one soup), an apple, a pear, a banana, a copy of a paperback book called *Death in the Desert*, a make-it-yourself record of Chris singing his song about the moon, a meat pie, an identity disc with Mortimer's name and address printed on it, a photograph of Arabel with Mortimer in his trumpet on her shoulder, a card saying that Chris weighed ten stone and would marry a dark girl and have six children, a vitamin C tablet, and two mentholated throat lozenges. Also Arabel had had her nose blown and Mortimer his feet massaged, which astonished him very much indeed.

'That's all,' said Arabel regretfully when they had put the mentholated throat lozenges into the empty cup which had held tomato soup. 'Could we start again?'

'No, we ought to go home,' said Chris. 'It must be your bedtime by now.'

'We could wake Uncle Arthur and ask him the time in case it isn't.'

'No, don't, he looks so peaceful. Come on, we can make some hot chocolate when we get back.'

They pulled Mortimer out of the tube station on his truck and started down the hill. The two men who had been waiting outside got back into their sports car and followed.

But Mortimer, when he found that the evening's entertainment was finished, became very despondent.

He began to grumble inside the trumpet, and to mutter, and flap his wings, or try to, and kick the carton of paraffin, and shout, 'Nevermore!' in a loud angry voice.

'He's upset because *he* didn't have a chance to put a coin in a machine,' said Arabel.

'He shouldn't have got inside my trumpet.'

'If we could only get it off him,' said Arabel, 'we could turn down Lykewake Lane and go home that way. There's a draper's shop that has a machine outside that you put fivepence in and it sews a button on while you wait.'

'Who wants a button sewn on?'

'Mortimer might like one on his face towel.'

'Oh, all right.'

So they turned down Lykewake Lane (just missing one of the gaggles of ladies and the fire engine cruising along the High Street) and the two men followed them in their sports car.

When they came to the draper's shop, which was called Cotton & Button, Arabel said,

'Mortimer. Will you stop shouting 'Nevermore' and listen. We are going to pull the trumpet off you, if we can, and then you can put fivepence in this machine for it to sew on a button.'

Silence from inside the trumpet while Mortimer thought about this.

'Do you think we really ought to pour paraffin on him?' said Chris. 'It might be bad for him. And it will make my trumpet smell terrible.'

'Well,' said Arabel, 'if you don't think we ought, Pa told me there's an Italian grocer's shop in Highgate that has an olive-oil machine.'

'I'm not walking all the way over to Highgate.'

'In that case we'll have to use paraffin,' said Arabel. 'Mortimer, we are going to turn you upside down and pour a little paraffin into the trumpet so as to loosen you and pull you out. Will you please try not to struggle?'

Silence.

Arabel picked up the trumpet and turned it upside down. Chris picked up the paraffin container.

At this moment the two men who had been following got out of their sports car and came quietly up beside them. Both were holding guns.

'Hold it, sonny,' said the one called Sid. 'That's a valuable bird you've got in that trumpet. Don't you go pouring paraffin down it or you might spoil him.'

'We know he's valuable,' said Arabel. 'He's my raven, Mortimer.'

'How are we going to get him out if we don't?' said Chris.

'Why are you holding guns?' said Arabel. 'You look rather silly.'

'That bird's no raven. That bird is a valuable mynah bird, the property of Slick Sim Symington, the Soho property millionaire. That bird was kidnapped last week by a rival gang – by a rival establishment – and it is our intention to get possession of him again. So hand him over.'

'Hand over Mortimer?' said Arabel. 'Not likely! Why he's my very own raven, he loves me, and he certainly isn't a miner bird, whatever they are.'

'We'll soon see about that,' said Bill. Putting his gun down on the red truck he grabbed hold of the trumpet with both hands while Sid, putting down *his* gun, grabbed Mortimer's feet.

There was a short, sharp struggle during which it was hard to see what was going on. Then the scene cleared, to show Mortimer sitting on Arabel's shoulder. His face towel had come off. The trumpet was on the ground. The two men were both bleeding freely from a number of wounds.

'Nevermore,' said Mortimer.

'*I'll say* it's nevermore,' said Bill. 'That's no mynah bird.'

'What a demon,' said Sid. 'Lucky he missed my jugular! You're right, miss, he's a raven, and all I can say is, I wish you joy of the nasty brute.'

'Very sorry you were troubled,' said Bill. 'Here, come on, Sid, let's get over to Rumbury General *quick*, and have us some anti-tetanus injections before we're rolling around like the exhibits in one of those kinetic shows.'

They jumped into their sports car and roared off, just missing the fire engine as they turned into the High Street.

'Hey,' Arabel called after them. 'You've left your guns behind.'

But it was too late, they were gone.

'Oh well,' said Arabel, 'perhaps, they'll call in for the guns tomorrow. Anyway, Mortimer, now you can sew on some buttons. We've got eighteen fivepenny pieces left.'

So Mortimer, jumping up and down with satisfaction and enthusiasm, put eighteen coins into the slot machine and it sewed seventeen buttons on to the face towel. (One of the coins turned out to be an old halfpenny with a hole in it.) Then they went home and let themselves in with Arabel's key.

They tidied up the kitchen and the airing cupboard. Chris mopped the floor. Then he made a saucepan full of hot chocolate while Arabel had a bath, and he brought her a mugful in bed, and she drank it. Then she had to get out of bed again to brush her teeth. Then she went to sleep.

Mortimer had already gone to sleep in the coal scuttle. He was tired out. Chris put all the cartons of milk except the one they had used for chocolate into the fridge, with the ham sandwich, the meat pie, the wine gums, the chocolate bars and the mentholated lozenges; he put the apple, pear and paperback book on the dresser, and the paraffin outside in the shed. He ate the banana.

He did not know what to do with the guns, so he left them on Arabel's red truck.

Then he put his do-it-yourself record on the record player and sat down to listen.

'*Morning moon, trespassing down over my skylight's shoulder,*
Who asked you in, to doodle across my deep-seated dream?'

At that moment the front door burst open and in rushed Mr and Mrs Jones, police, firemen and a lot of ladies with blankets and tea.

'Arabel? Oh, where's my child?' cried Mrs Jones, when she saw Chris.

'Where's the gorillas?' asked Mrs Finney.

'And the mambas?' asked Mr Finney.

'And this here gang of Arabian Knights?' said Sergeant Pike.

'Arabel? Why, she's asleep in bed,' said Chris, puzzled. 'Where else would she be? You're back early, aren't you?'

Mrs Jones ran up the stairs.

Sure enough, there was Arabel, asleep in bed.

'What about Mortimer?'

'He's asleep in the coal scuttle.'

There was a long, long silence while everybody gazed about at the tidy kitchen.

At last Mr Jones said, 'What's that guitar doing up on top of the broom cupboard?'

'I put it up there to be out of Mortimer's reach,' said Chris. 'He wanted to look for diamonds inside it.'

'He does do that sometimes,' Mr Jones said, nodding.

After another long silence Sergeant Pike said, 'If you ask *me*, everybody in this room has been suffering from one of them mass delusions. If you ask *me*, we'd better all forget about this evening's occurrences and go home to bed.'

Nobody disagreed. They all filed silently out of Mrs Jones's kitchen and out of the house. Mr Finney muttered,

'Maybe there *was* an escape of gas and it sort of affected everybody's mind. Or maybe it was food poisoning. Those crisps at the Assembly Rooms weren't very fresh.'

Mr and Mrs Jones paid Chris his babysitting fee and he went home. Then they went, to bed. They were almost as tired as Mortimer.

Next day, when Mr Jones had gone off to drive his taxi, Mrs Jones said to Arabel,

'What's all this milk doing in the fridge, and this meat pie and ham sandwich?'

'We'd used up all the milk so we went and got some more from the automatic machine.'

'Did you go out after your bedtime?'

'No, it was twenty-five past eight. We got some other things from automatic machines too. The pie is a present for Pa, and that book is a present for you.'

Mrs Jones looked at the paperback called *Death in the Desert*. It had a picture of a person tied to a railway line.

'Thank you, dearie. I'll read it sometime when I'm not busy,' she said, and put it on a high shelf of the dresser. Then she said, 'Where did those toy guns come from?'

'I don't think they are toys,' said Arabel. 'They belong to two men, I think they were miners, who thought Mortimer was an escaped miner's bird. But they soon saw he wasn't.'

'Funny,' said Mrs Jones. 'But I believe I did hear they used birds in the mines to smell if there's a gas escape. I didn't know miners had to carry guns, though. Oh well, I daresay they'll come back for them.'

She put the guns on another high shelf.

For a long time after that, people in Rumbury Town talked about the evening when the deadly black mamba escaped from the gasworks.

Mrs Jones was so pleased to have back her pearl-handled knives and forks that she forgave Arabel for the seventeen buttons sewn on the face towel, and the strip torn off it.

Mortimer slept in the coal scuttle for seventeen hours. Then he woke up and began digging for diamonds. He threw all the coal out of the coal scuttle on to the kitchen hearthrug, lump by lump.

But he did not find any diamonds.

The Bread Bin

ALL THIS HAPPENED one terrible wild, wet week in February when Mortimer the raven had been living with Arabel Jones in Rainwater Crescent for several months.

The weather had been so dreadful for so long that everybody in the Jones family was, if not in a bad temper, at least less cheerful than usual. Mrs Jones complained that even the bread felt damp unless it was made into toast. Arabel had the beginnings of a cold, Mr Jones found it very tiring having to drive his taxi through pouring rain along greasy, skiddy streets day after day, and Mortimer was annoyed because there were two things he wanted to do, and he was not permitted to do either of them. He wanted to be given a ride round the garden in Arabel's red truck (Mrs Jones would not allow it because of the weather) and he wanted to climb into the bread bin and go to sleep there. It seemed to him very unreasonable that he wasn't allowed to do this.

'We could keep the bread somewhere else,' Arabel said.

'So I buy a bread bin that costs me ninety-five new pence for a great, fat, sulky, lazy bird to sleep in? What's wrong with the coal scuttle? He's slept in *that* for the last three weeks!'

Mrs Jones had just come back from shopping, very wet. She began taking groceries from her tartan wheeled shopping bag and dumping them out on the kitchen floor.

'He wants a change,' said Arabel, looking out of the window at the grey lines of rain that went slamming across the garden like telephone wires.

'Oh naturally! Ginger marmalade on crumpets that bird gets for his breakfast, spaghetti and meatballs for lunch, brandy snaps for supper, allowed to sit inside the grandfather clock *and* slide down the stairs on my best tray with the painted pink and green gladioli and he must have a *change*, as well? That bird gets more attention than the Lord Mayor of Hyderabad.'

'He doesn't know that,' said Arabel. 'He hasn't been to Hyderabad.'

Arabel and Mortimer went into the front hall. Arabel balanced Mortimer on one of her roller skates and tied a bit of string to it and pulled him around the downstairs part of the house. But neither of them cheered up much. Arabel's throat felt tight and tickly and Mortimer rode along with his head sunk down between his shoulders and his beak sunk down into his chest among his feathers, and his feathers all higgledy-piggledy, as if he didn't care which way they pointed.

The telephone rang.

Mortimer would have liked to answer it – he loved answering the telephone – but he had one of his toenails caught in the roller skate; kicking and flapping to free himself he started the skate rolling, shot across the kitchen, knocked over Mrs Jones's vegetable rack (which had four pounds of Brussels sprouts in the top basket), and cannoned against a sack of coffee beans and a brand new container

of oven spray, which began shooting out a thick frothy foam. A fierce white smoke came boiling off the foam which made everyone cough. Mrs Jones rushed to open the window. A lot of wind and rain blew in, knocking over a jar of plastic daffodils from the windowsill, and Mortimer quickly pushed some under the kitchen mat; sliding things underneath mats or linoleum was one of his favourite hobbies.

The phone went on ringing.

Suddenly Mortimer noticed the open window; he climbed up the handles of the drawers under the kitchen sink, very fast, claw over claw, scrabbled his way along the side of the sink, up on to the windowsill, and looked out into the wild, wet, windy garden.

'Drat that phone!' said Mrs Jones, and rushed to answer it. But just as she got there the phone stopped ringing.

Leaning out of the window Mortimer could see that Arabel's red truck was just outside the window, down below on the grass, with two inches of rain in it.

'Mortimer!' said Arabel. 'Come back! You'll get wet.'

Mortimer took no notice. There were half a dozen horse chestnuts floating in the red truck.

The next-door cat, Ginger, was sitting under a wheelbarrow, trying to keep dry. Mortimer jumped out into the truck (up to his black, feathery knees in water), and began throwing chestnuts at Ginger. He was a very good shot.

'Mortimer!' said Arabel, hanging out of the window. 'You are not to throw conkers at Ginger. He's never done you any harm.'

Mortimer took no notice. He threw another conker.

Arabel wriggled back off the draining board, opened the back door, ran out into the garden, grabbed the handle of the truck, and pulled it back indoors with Mortimer on board.

Some of the water slopped on to the kitchen floor, sending a tidal wave of coffee beans and Brussel sprouts towards the hall.

'*Arabel!*' said Mrs Jones, coming back into the kitchen. 'Have you been out of doors in your bedroom slippers? Oh my stars, if you don't catch your mortal end my name's Mrs Gipsy Petulengro. And where's all this water come from?'

'I had to fetch Mortimer, because he was getting wet,' said Arabel. 'I stayed on the path.'

'Getting wet?' said Mrs Jones. 'Why shouldn't he get wet? Birds are *meant* to get wet, that's why

they have feathers. I suppose we should dry him off with the hairdryer?'

She shoved the truck outside, skidding on sprouts and coffee beans, and slammed the door.

The phone began to ring once more.

Arabel thought the hairdryer was a good idea. While Mrs Jones hurried back to the telephone, she got the dryer out of its box, plugged it in, and started blowing Mortimer dry. All his feathers stood straight up, making him look like a turkey. He was so astonished that he shouted, 'Nevermore!' and stepped backwards into a tray of bread rolls

that were waiting to go into the oven. He sank
into them up to his ankles and left bird's-claw
footprints all along them. But he enjoyed being
dried and turned round and round so that
Arabel could blow him all over, and between
every feather.

'That was Auntie Brenda,' said Mrs Jones,
coming back after a long chat. 'She says she's
taking her lot roller-skating at the rink, and she'll
stop by and pick us up too.'

'Oh,' said Arabel.

'Don't you *want* to go roller-skating?' said
Mrs Jones.

'Well, I expect Mortimer will enjoy it,' said
Arabel.

'I just hope he doesn't disgrace us,' said
Mrs Jones, giving Mortimer an old-fashioned
look. 'But I'm not going out and leaving him alone

in the house. Never shall I forget, not if I should live to eighty and be elected Beauty Queen of the Home Counties, the time we went to the *Babes in the Wood* and when we got back he'd eaten the banisters and the bathroom basin complete, and two-and-a-half packets of assorted Rainbow Bath Oil Bubble Gums.'

'Nevermore,' said Mortimer.

'Promises, promises,' said Mrs Jones.

'The house looked lovely, all full of bubbles,' Arabel said. 'Mortimer thought so too.'

'Anyway he's not having the chance to do it again. Put your coat on; Auntie Brenda will be here in ten minutes.'

Arabel put her coat on slowly. Her throat tickled more and more; she did not feel in the least like going out. Also, although they were her cousins, she was not very fond of Aunt Brenda's lot. There were three of them: their names were Lindy, Cindy and Mindy. As a matter of fact, they were horrible girls. They had unkind natures and liked to say things on purpose to hurt other people's feelings. They were always eating, not because they were hungry, but just because they were greedy. They pestered their mother for choc ices and bags of crisps and bottles of Coke all the time they were out. They had more toys than they could be bothered to play with. And they had a lot of spots too.

They had not yet met Mortimer.

Aunt Brenda stopped outside the house in her shiny new car.

Cindy, Lindy and Mindy put their heads out of the window and stopped eating chocolate macaroni sticks long enough to scream,

'Hallo, Arabel! We've got new coats, new boots, new furry hoods, new furry gloves, new skirts, and new roller skates!'

'Spoilt lot,' muttered Mrs Jones, putting Arabel's old skates in her tartan wheeled shopping bag. 'So what was wrong with the old ones, I should like to know? Anyone would think their dad was the president of the Bank of Monte Carlo.'

In fact, their dad was a salesman in do-it-yourself wardrobe kits; he travelled so much that he was hardly ever at home.

Arabel went out to the car in her old coat, old hood, old gloves and old boots. She held Mortimer tightly. He was very interested when he caught sight of the car; his black eyes shone like black satin buttons.

'We're going in that car, Mortimer,' Arabel said to him.

'Kaaaark,' said Mortimer.

Lindy and Cindy hung out of the back window shouting, 'Arabel, Arabel, 'orrible Arabel, 'orrible 'orrible, 'orrible Arabel.' Then they spotted Mortimer and their eyes went as round as LP records.

'Coo!' said Cindy. 'What's *that*?'

'What *have* you got there, 'orrible Arabel?' said Lindy.

'He's my raven, Mortimer,' said Arabel.

All three girls burst into screams of laughter.

'A raven? What d'you want a *raven* for? Anyway, he's not a raven – he's just a rusty old rook!'

'A junky old jackdaw!'

'What's the use of him, can he talk?'

'If he wants to,' said Arabel.

Cindy, Lindy and Mindy laughed even louder.

'I bet all he can say is caw! See, saw, old Jacky Daw. All he can do is croak and caw!'

'Stop teasing, girls, and make room for Arabel in the back,' said Auntie Brenda.

Arabel and Mortimer got into the back and sat quietly there without saying anything more. Cindy tried to give Mortimer's tail feathers a tweak, but he turned his head right round on its rusty black neck and looked at her so fiercely that she changed her mind.

Mrs Jones got into the front beside her sister Brenda, and they were off.

Mortimer had never been in a car before. He liked it. As soon as he had made sure that Arabel's cousins were not going to attack him at once, he began to bounce up and down gently on Arabel's shoulder, looking out at the shops of Rumbury High Street flashing past, at the red buses swishing along, at the street lamps like a string of salmon-coloured daisies, the scarlet letter boxes, and the greengrocer's all red and orange and yellow and green.

'Nevermore,' he muttered. 'Nevermore.'

'There, you see,' said Arabel: 'He *can* speak.'

'But what does he mean?' giggled Mindy.

'He means that where he comes from they don't have buses and greengrocers and street lamps and letter boxes.'

'Oh, what rubbish! I don't believe you know what he means at all.'

After that Arabel kept quiet.

When they arrived at Rumbury Borough Roller Skating Rink Mortimer was even more amazed at the big sign above the entrance, all picked out in pink lights, and the forecourt, paved with yellow glass tiles.

'You get the tickets, Martha, I'll put the car in the car park,' said Auntie Brenda.

Arabel's three cousins were all expert roller skaters. They came to the rink two or three times every week. They buckled on their new skates and shot off into the middle, knocking over any amount of people on the way.

Arabel, when she had put on her skates, went slowly and carefully round the edge. She did not want to risk being knocked into because Mortimer was perched on her shoulder. Also she felt very tired and her throat had stopped tickling and was now really sore. And her feet were cold. And her head ached.

Auntie Brenda came back from putting away the car and sat down by Mrs Jones and the two sisters began talking their heads off.

'We'll have to stay here for hours yet,' thought Arabel.

'Come on into the middle, cowardy custard!
Caw, caw, cowardy, cowardy!' screamed Lindy
and Cindy.

'Yes, go on, ducky, you'll be all right, there's
nothing to be afraid of,' called Auntie Brenda.
But Arabel shook her head and stuck to the edge.

Mortimer was having a lovely time. He didn't
mind Arabel going so slowly because he was
looking around at all the other skaters. He admired
the way they whizzed in and out and round and
through and past and in and out and round. He
dug his claws lovingly into Arabel's shoulder.

'I wish I had three roller skates, Mortimer,' Arabel said. 'Then you could sit on one and ride.'

Mortimer wished it too.

'I'll tell you what,' Arabel said. 'I'll take my skates off. I don't feel much like skating.'

She sat down at the edge, took her skates off, carried one, and lifted Mortimer on to the other, which she pulled along by the laces.

'Cooo!' shrieked Cindy, whirling past. 'Look at scaredy-baby Arabel, pulling her silly old rook along.'

'Round the ritzy rink the ragged rookie rolls,' screeched Mindy.

'Scared to skate, scared to skate,' chanted Lindy.

They really were horrible girls.

Arabel went very slowly over to where her mother and Auntie Brenda were sitting.

'Can I go home, please, Ma?' she said. 'My legs ache.'

'Oh, go on, ducky, have another try,' said Auntie Brenda cheerfully. 'There's nothing to be scared of, really there isn't. You've got to fall over a few times before you learn.'

But Mrs Jones looked carefully at her daughter and said, 'Don't you feel well, dearie?'

'No,' said Arabel, and two tears rolled slowly down her cheeks. Mrs Jones put a hand on Arabel's forehead.

'It's quite hot,' she said. 'I think we'd better go home, Brenda.'

'Oh my goodness,' said Auntie Brenda rather crossly. 'Can't she stay another half hour?'

Mrs Jones shook her head. 'I don't think she ought.'

'Oh dear, the girls *will* be disappointed.' Brenda raised her voice in a terrific shout. 'Cindy! Lindy! Miiiiindy! Come along – your cousin's not feeling well.'

Arabel's three cousins came dragging slowly across the rink with sulky expressions.

'*Now* what?' said Mindy.

'We only just got here,' said Cindy.

'Just because 'orrible Arabel can't skate –' said Lindy.

'Ma, can't you and I go home by bus?' said Arabel.

Auntie Brenda and the three girls looked hopeful, but Mrs Jones shook her head, 'I really think we ought to get home as quickly as possible. Besides, I've left my shopping bag in the boot of your car, Brenda.'

'Oh, very well,' said Brenda impatiently. 'Come along, girls.'

The girls took their skates off very slowly and they all trailed off to the car park, which was the multistorey kind. Aunt Brenda's car was up on the fourth level.

'Not worth waiting for the lift,' Brenda said. So they walked up.

They had to climb a lot of steps. Arabel's legs ached worse and worse. But Mortimer was even more interested by the car park than he had been by the skating rink. Arabel was carrying him, and her skates. Mortimer gazed around with astonishment at the huge concrete slopes, and the huge level stretches, dotted with red and black and blue and orange and silver cars.

Mortimer's eyes sparkled like blackcurrant wine gums. Arabel's arms ached almost as much as her legs. While Auntie Brenda was rummaging for her car key at the bottom of her cluttered handbag, Arabel put her skates down on the ground.

With a quick wriggle, Mortimer slid from Arabel's grasp and stepped on to one of her skates. Then he half spread his wings and gave himself a mighty shove-off. The roller skate, with Mortimer sitting on it, went whizzing with the speed of a

Vampire jet along the flat concrete runway, between two rows of parked cars.

'Oh, stop him, stop him!' Arabel said. 'He'll go down the ramp!'

She meant to shout, but the words only came out in a whisper.

Lindy, Mindy and Cindy rushed after Mortimer. But they were too late to catch him. He shot down the ramp on to the third level.

'Nevermore, nevermore, nevermore, *nevermore*!' he shouted joyfully, and gave himself another shove with his wings, which sent him up the ramp on the opposite side, and back on to the fourth level.

'There he goes, there!' cried Auntie Brenda. 'After him, girls!' But Lindy, Mindy and Cindy were now out of earshot, down on the third level.

'Oh goodness gracious me, did you ever see anything so outrageously provoking in all your born *days*,' said Mrs Jones. 'I never did, not even when I worked at the Do-It-Yourself Delicatessen! Don't you go running after that black feathered monster, Arabel, you stay right here.'

But Arabel had toiled after Mortimer up on to the fifth level.

'Mortimer! Please come back!' she called in her voice that would not come out any louder than a whisper. '*Please* come back. I don't feel very well. I'll bring you here again another day.'

Mortimer didn't hear her.

Up on the fifth level the wind was icy, and whistled like a saw blade. Arabel began to shiver and couldn't stop.

Mortimer was having a wonderful time, shooting up and down ramps, in and out between cars, rowing himself along with his wings at a terrific rate. Other car owners began running after him.

'Stop that bird!' shouted Auntie Brenda. Lots of people tried. But Mortimer was going so fast that it was easy for him to dodge them; he had discovered the knack of steering the roller skate with his tail, and he spun round corners and in between people's legs, umbrellas and shopping

baskets as if he were entered for the All-Europe Raven Bobsleigh Finals.

After ten minutes there must have been at least fifty people chasing from one ramp to another, all over the multistorey car park.

In the end Mortimer was caught quite by chance when a stoutly built lady, who had just come in from the outside stairs, stuck out her umbrella to twirl the rain off it before closing it; Mortimer, swinging round a Ford Capri on one wheel, ran full tilt into the umbrella and found himself tangled among the spokes. By the time he was disentangled, Auntie Brenda, very cross, had come up and seized him by the scruff of his neck.

'*Now* perhaps we can get going,' she snapped, and carried him kicking back to her car. 'He can go in your shopper, Martha,' she said grimly, 'then he won't be able to give any more trouble. I really don't know why you wanted to come to the roller rink with a *raven*.'

Mrs Jones was too anxious about Arabel to answer.

Presently Lindy, Cindy and Mindy came panting and straggling back, and Arabel walked slowly up from the third level. She couldn't stop shivering.

'Where's Mortimer?' she whispered.

'He's in the boot and there he'll stay till you get home,' said Auntie Brenda. 'That bird's in disgrace.'

Arabel started to say, 'He didn't know he was doing anything wrong. He thought the car park was a skating rink for ravens,' but the words stuck inside, as if her throat was full of grit.

By the time they arrived at the Jones's house, Number Six, Rainwater Crescent, Arabel was crying as well as shivering.

She couldn't seem to stop doing either of those things.

Mrs Jones jumped out of the car and almost carried Arabel into the house.

'Your shopper!' Auntie Brenda shouted after them, getting the tartan bag out of the boot.

'Leave it in the front hall, Brenda.'

Brenda did. But she and Martha had exactly similar bags on wheels. They had bought them together at a grand clearance sale in Rumbury Bargain Basement Bazaar. Brenda put the wrong bag in the front hall. She left the one that still contained Mortimer in her car boot. Besides Mortimer, it held two pounds of ripe bananas. Mortimer, who loved bananas and wasn't usually allowed as many as he would have liked, was too busy eating them just then to complain about being shut inside the bag.

'We'd better get home quick,' Auntie Brenda said. 'We won't hang about in case Arabel's got something catching.'

She had to make three stops on the way home in any case, however, for Cindy wanted a Dairy Isobar, Lindy wanted a Hokey-Coke, and Mindy wanted a bag of Chewy Gooeys. All these had to be bought at different shops. By the time they reached Auntie Brenda's house Mortimer had finished the bananas and was ready to be unzipped from the tartan bag.

When Auntie Brenda undid the zip, expecting to see two raspberry dairy bricks, half a dozen hundred-watt light bulbs, and a head of celery, out shot Mortimer, leaving behind him an utter tangle of empty rinds and squashed banana pulp.

'Oh, my dear cats alive!' said Auntie Brenda. Mortimer was so smothered in banana pulp that for a moment she did not even recognize him. Then she cried, 'Girls! It's that awful bird of Arabel's. Quick! Catch the nasty brute. He needs teaching a lesson, that bird does.'

Lindy snatched up a walking stick, Cindy got a tennis racket, and Mindy found a shrimping net left over from last summer at Prittlewell on Sea. They started chasing Mortimer all over their house. Mortimer never flew if he could help it; he preferred walking at a dignified pace; but just now it seemed best to fly. Getting his wings to open was difficult at first, because of all the mashed banana, but he managed it. He flew to the drawing-room mantelpiece. Mindy took a swipe at him with her shrimping net and knocked off the clock under its glass dome. Mortimer managed to flap to the hanging light in the middle of the room and dangled from it upside down, shaking off bits of banana. Cindy whirled her tennis racket and sent the light flying through the window, bulb shade and all. Mortimer landed on to the top of the bookshelf. Lindy tried to hook

him with her walking stick and smashed the glass front of the bookcase.

'Use your hands, nincompoops,' shouted Auntie Brenda. 'You're breaking the place up.'

So they dropped their sticks and rackets and nets and went after Mortimer with their hands. Mortimer never, never pecked Arabel. But then she never tried to pull his tail, or grab him by the leg, or snatch hold of his wing; fairly soon Cindy, Lindy and Mindy were covered with peck marks and bleeding quite freely here and there.

Aunt Brenda tried throwing a tablecloth over Mortimer. That didn't work. She knocked over a table lamp and a jar of chrysanthemums. But after a long chase she managed to get him cornered in the fireplace. The fire was not lit.

Mortimer went up the chimney.

'Now we've got him,' said Auntie Brenda.

'He'll fly out of the top,' said Lindy.

'He can't, there's a cowl on it,' said Cindy.

They could hear Mortimer, scrabbling in the chimney and muttering, 'Nevermore,' to himself.

Auntie Brenda telephoned the sweep, whose name was Ephraim Suckett, and asked him to come round right away.

In ten minutes he arrived, full of curiosity, with his long flexible rods, and his brushes, and his huge vacuum cleaner.

'Been having a party?' he asked, as he looked around the drawing room. 'Wonderful larks these teenagers do get up to.'

'We've got a bird in the chimney,' Aunt Brenda said grimly. 'I want you to get him out.'

'A bird, eh?' said Mr Suckett cautiously, looking at the damage. 'He wouldn't be one o' them Anacondors with a wing spread of twenty foot? If so I want extra cover in advance under my Industrial Injuries Policy.'

'He's an ordinary, common raven,' snapped Auntie Brenda, 'and I'd like you to get him out of that chimney as quickly as possible. I want to light the fire before my husband gets home.'

So Mr Suckett poked one of his rods up the chimney as far as it would go, and then screwed another one on to the bottom and poked that up, and then screwed another one on to *that*. A lot of soot fell into the hearth.

'When did you last have this chimney swept?' Mr Suckett asked. 'Coronation year?'

Mortimer retired further up the chimney.

Meanwhile, what had happened to Arabel?

She had gone to the hospital.

Mrs Jones rang the doctor as soon as she was indoors. The doctor came quickly and said that Arabel had a nasty case of bronchitis and would be better off in Rumbury Central, so Mr Jones, who had just arrived home for his tea, drove her there at once in his taxi, wrapped up in three pink blankets, with her feet on a hot-water bottle.

'Where's Mortimer? Is he all right?' Arabel asked faintly in the taxi. 'What about his tea?'

'Your pa'll give him his tea when he gets home,' said Mrs Jones. She had clean forgotten Mortimer was still in her tartan shopping bag.

Mr Jones left his wife and daughter at the hospital and drove sadly home. In the front hall he found a tartan shopping bag containing two raspberry dairy bricks, some electric light bulbs, and a head of celery. He put these things away. 'Wonder why Martha got all those light bulbs?' he thought. 'She must know there are plenty in the tool cupboard.'

Feeling rather hungry, he made himself a pot of tea and a large dish of spaghetti in cheese sauce, which was the only thing he knew how to cook. Then it struck him that the house was unusually quiet. Normally when Mortimer was awake there would be a scrunching, or a scraping, or a tapping, or a tinkling, as the raven carefully took something to pieces, or knocked something over to see if it would break, or pushed one thing under some other thing to see if it would go.

'Mortimer?' called Mr Jones. 'Where are you?' No answer. 'Come out!'

There was still no answer. Nobody said, 'Nevermore.' The house remained quite silent.

Mr Jones began to feel anxious. In his own way, he was fond of Mortimer. Also he wanted to be sure the raven was not eating the back wall of the house, or unravelling the bath towels (Mortimer could take a whole bath towel to pieces in three

and a half minutes flat), or munching up the
Home Handyman's Encyclopedia in ten volumes.
Or anything else.

High and low Mr Jones hunted all over the
house for Mortimer and didn't find him anywhere.

'Oh my goodness,' he thought. 'The bird must
have wandered out unbeknowst while we were
getting Arabel into the taxi. She will be terribly
upset. How shall we ever be able to break it to
her? She thinks the world of that bird.'

Just at that moment the telephone rang.

When Mr Jones picked the phone up, words
came out of it in a solid shriek.

'What's that?' said Mr Jones, listening. 'Who is
it? This is Jones's Taxi Service here. Is that *you*,
Brenda? Is something the matter?'

The shrieking went on. All Mr Jones could distinguish was something about chrysanthemums, and something about soot, and something about a clock.

'Soot in the clock,' he thought. 'That's unusual. Maybe they've got an oil-fired clock, I daresay such things do exist, and Brenda's always been dead keen on the latest gadgets.'

'I can't help you, Brenda, I'm afraid,' he said into the telephone. 'I don't know much about oil-fired clocks, matter of fact, nothing at all. You'll have to wait till Arthur gets home. We're all at sixes and sevens here because Arabel's gone to the hospital.' And he rang off; he felt he had more things to worry about than soot in his sister-in-law's clock.

Meanwhile, what had been happening to Mortimer?

Mr Suckett, the sweep, had fastened more and more rods together and poked them further and further up Brenda's chimney. Mortimer had retired right up to the very top, but he couldn't get out because of the cowl, though he could look out through the slits. He had a good view and found it very interesting, for Brenda's house was right on top of Rumbury Hill and he could see for miles – all the way over Rumbury Heath and down across London as far as the Houses of Parliament. Auntie Brenda's chimney was unusually high.

Mr Suckett had his big vacuum cleaner switched on, and he was sucking up the bales and bales of soot that kept tumbling down the chimney as Mortimer climbed higher and higher.

At last, finding that he could not dislodge Mortimer with his rods, Mr Suckett began pulling them down again and unscrewing them one by one.

'What'll you do now?' asked Lindy.

'Will you have to take the top of the chimney off?' said Mindy.

'Shall we light a fire and toast him?' said Cindy.

'Just get rid of him *somehow* and be quick about it,' said Auntie Brenda.

'We'll have to suck him out,' said the sweep.

He withdrew the last of his rods and wheeled the vacuum cleaner close to the fireplace.

This cleaner was like an ordinary household one, but about eight times larger. It had a big canvas drum on wheels, into which all the soot was sucked. When he had finished a job, Mr Suckett took it away and sold the soot to people at fifty-nine pence a pound to put on their slugs. Better than orange peel, he said it was.

By now the canvas drum was packed to bursting with all the soot that had been in Auntie Brenda's chimney, piling up since Coronation year.

Mr Suckett shoved the nozzle up the chimney and switched on the motor.

It had a tremendously powerful suck. It could yank a St Bernard dog right off its feet and up a ten-foot ramp at an angle of thirty degrees against a force six wind. It sucked Mortimer down the chimney like one of his own feathers.

He shot down the chimney, along the canvas tube, and ended up inside the canvas drum, stuffed in with a hundredweight of soot.

Mortimer had quite enjoyed being in the chimney where, if dark, it was interesting; besides, there was the view from the top.

But he did not at all enjoy being sucked down so fast – upside down as it happened – still less did he like being packed into a bag full of suffocating black powder.

He began to kick and flap and peck and shout 'Nevermore' and in less time than it takes to tell he had jabbed and clawed a huge hole in the side of the canvas drum; he burst out through this hole like a black bombshell and a hundredweight of soot followed him out.

Auntie Brenda had opened all the windows when Mr Suckett began poking his rods up the chimney, to get rid of the smell of soot, which made her feel faint. Mortimer went out through a window with the speed of a Boeing 707; he had had enough of Auntie Brenda's house.

He left a scene of such blackness and muddle behind him that I do not really think it would be worth trying to describe it.

As soon as Mortimer was a short distance away from the house he glided down to the ground and set off walking. He really disapproved of flying. He had no idea where Auntie Brenda's house was, nor where Arabel's house was but this didn't worry him. Since Auntie Brenda's house was on the top of a hill he walked downhill, and he studied each front door as he passed it in hopes it would seem familiar. None did, so he went on, rather slowly.

Mr Jones was at home, about to start his spaghetti, and wondering if he should call up the hospital to ask how Arabel was getting on, when the telephone rang.

It was Mrs Jones.

'Is that you, Ben?' she said. 'Oh dear, Ben, poor Arabel's ever so ill, tossing and turning and deliriated, and she keeps asking for Mortimer, and the doctor said it will be all right this once and you'd better bring him in case the sight of him might do her good.'

Mr Jones's heart fell into his sheepskin slippers.

'Mortimer's not here,' he said.

'Not *there*? Whatever do you mean, Ben, he must be there.' Then for the first time Mrs Jones remembered and let out a guilty gulp. 'Oh bless my soul, whatever will I forget next? I quite forgot that poor bird, though gracious knows the bother he caused with the coffee beans and the conkers and the car park. Anyhow a couple of hours shut up in a bag is no more than he deserves for all his troublesomeness, but you'd better let him out right away, poor thing.'

'Let him out of *where*?'

'My zip tartan bag. He's inside it.'

'No, he's not, Martha,' said Mr Jones. 'There was a head of celery, two raspberry family dairy bricks, and half a dozen hundred-watt bulbs. What did you want to get all those for; we had plenty already?'

Mrs Jones let out another squawk. 'Oh my stars, then he must be at Brenda's. She must have taken the wrong bag by mistake. You'd better go right round there and fetch him, Ben, and bring him to the hospital. And when you come, bring two more of Arabel's nighties, and a packet of teabags, and my digestive mint lozenges.'

'Round at Brenda's, is he?' said Mr Jones slowly. A lot of things began to make sense: the soot and the clock and the chrysanthemums. 'All right, Martha, I'll go and get him and bring him as fast as I can.'

He did not tell Martha about the clock and the chrysanthemums. He hung up and then dialled Brenda's number.

There was no reply. In fact, her line seemed to be out of order, he could hear a kind of muffled sound at the other end, but that was all.

It wasn't hard to guess that if there had been some kind of trouble at Brenda's house, then Mortimer was somehow connected with that trouble.

Mr Jones scratched his head. Then he took off his slippers and put on his shoes and overcoat again. Sighing, he drove his taxi out of its shed and slowly up to where Rainwater Crescent meets Rumbury High Street. There are four traffic lights at this junction, or should be; this evening they did not seem to be working.

The traffic was in a horrible tangle, two policemen were trying to sort it out, and a third was inspecting, with the help of a torch, the chewed stumps like celery sticks that were all that was left of the traffic lights.

'Evening, Sid,' said Mr Jones, putting his head out of the cab window. 'What's going on?'

'Oh, hallo, Ben, is that you? Well, you'll think I'm barmy, but someone seems to have eaten the traffic lights.'

'Oh,' said Mr Jones.

He backed his cab fifty yards down the Crescent again, and got out.

'Mortimer!' he shouted. 'Where are you?'

'Nevermore,' said a voice at ankle level in the dark behind him. Although he had been expecting something of the kind, Mr Jones jumped. Then he turned round and saw Mortimer, with his eyes shining in the light of the street lamps, walking slowly along by the hedge, peering in at all the front gates of the houses as he came to them. He was on the wrong side of the street, so it was

likely that he would have passed clean by Number Six and gone on goodness knows where.

Mr Jones picked him up. Mortimer was covered in soot, and with two pounds of bananas inside him, he weighed as much as the London Telephone Directory.

'I daresay I ought to turn you over to the police for eating the traffic lights and causing an obstruction,' he said severely. 'But Arabel's ill in the hospital, so I'm going to take you to see her. And you'd better behave yourself.'

'Kaaaark,' said Mortimer. Mr Jones was not absolutely encouraged by the way he said it but there was no time to go into a lot of explanation about hospitals.

He hurried home, because he had not yet packed up the nightdresses, teabags and digestive mints. While he was doing all this, Mortimer wandered into the kitchen and saw the large dish of spaghetti that Mr Jones had cooked for his supper.

Mortimer looked at it thoughtfully. He loved spaghetti as a rule, but just at present he was so full that he felt unable to eat anything else.

'Nevermore,' he said sadly.

He wanted to make some use of the spaghetti, he didn't want it to go to waste, so he looked

around for a container. When allowed to do so, Mortimer greatly enjoyed packing spaghetti into jam jars or sponge bags or old yoghurt pots.

He had just disposed of the spaghetti when Mr Jones came hurrying back with the mints and nightdresses, took a box of teabags from the kitchen cupboard, dropped all these things into the tartan zip bag, put on his overcoat again, and picked up Mortimer. He did not notice the empty spaghetti dish.

By now it was quite late in the evening, but Mr Jones supposed that it would be all right to go to the hospital, although it was after visiting hours, since the doctor had told him to bring Mortimer.

He drove his taxi to Rumbury Central, parked it in the forecourt, and walked in with Mortimer on his shoulder.

Mortimer was amazed by the hospital. He liked it even better than the multistorey car-park. It had been built about a hundred years ago by Florence Nightingale, of black-pudding coloured brick, and was huge, like a prison. Its corridors were about a mile long, and it had ceilings so high that the smallest sound echoed like thunder. Many patients believed the nurses and doctors were allowed to drive cars along the passages, although this was not actually the case.

Mr Jones went up to the fourth floor in a great creaking lift as big as a post office – at which Mortimer said, 'Kaaark,' because it reminded him of the lift in Rumbury Tube Station. They walked along miles of green-floored passage until they found Balaclava Ward. There was nobody in sight to ask if he might go in, so Mr Jones stood on tiptoe with Mortimer on his shoulder and peered through two round glass holes like portholes in the ward doors. He could see a double row of white-covered beds and, halfway along, his wife Martha, sitting by one of them. He caught her eye and waved. She made signs that he was to wait until the Sister – who wore a white pie-frill cap and sat at a desk near the door – noticed him and let him in.

Mr Jones nodded.

He stuck his hands in his pockets and prepared to wait quietly.

But he didn't wait quietly. Instead, he let out a series of such piercing yells that patients shot bolt upright in their beds all over that wing of the hospital, porters rammed their trolleys into doors, nurses dropped trays of instruments, ambulances started up outside and rushed away, doctors jabbed themselves with syringes, and Mortimer, who had been sitting quietly, flew straight into the air and flapped distractedly round and round, shouting, 'Nevermore, nevermore, nevermore!'

Mr Jones fainted dead away on the floor.

Sister Bridget Hagerty came rushing out of the ward. She was small and black-haired and freckled; her eyes were as blue as blue scouring powder; when she gave orders for a thing to be done it was done right away. But everybody liked her.

'What in the name of goodness is going on here?' she snapped.

Dr Antonio arrived. He was in charge of that wing of the hospital at night and had just come on duty. He was not the same doctor who had told Mrs Jones to have Mortimer brought. In fact, Dr Antonio couldn't stand birds. He had been frightened by a tame cockatoo at the age of three, in his pram; ever since then the sight of any bird larger than a blue tit brought him out in a rash.

He came out in a rash now, bright scarlet, at the sight of Mortimer.

'It's obvious what's going on!' he said. 'That dangerous brute has attacked this poor fellow. Palgrave! Where are you?'

Palgrave was the ward orderly, who had gone to fetch the doctor a cup of instant coffee. He came running along the corridor at the doctor's shout.

'Palgrave, get that bird out of here at once.'

'Yes, sir, right away, sir,' said Palgrave, and he opened a window and threw the cup of hot coffee all over Mortimer, who was still circling around overhead, wondering what had come over Mr Jones.

Mortimer didn't care for coffee, unless it was very sweet, and his feelings were hurt; he flew out of the window.

'Doctor, there's something very funny about this man,' said Sister Bridget, who was kneeling by Mr Jones. 'Why do you suppose his hands are all covered with spaghetti in cheese sauce?'

'Perhaps he's an emergency burn case,' suggested the doctor. 'Perhaps he couldn't find anything else and used the spaghetti as a burn dressing. We had better take him along to Casualty. Palgrave, get a stretcher.'

'But his pockets are full of spaghetti too,' said Sister Bridget.

'Perhaps he was on his way to visit some Italian friends,' said Dr Antonio. 'Perhaps he *is* Italian. *Parla Italiano?*' he shouted hopefully into Mr Jones's ear.

Mr Jones groaned.

'*Parla Italiano?*' said the doctor again.

Mr Jones, who had flown over Italy as a Spitfire pilot in World War II, said feebly, 'Have we crashed? Where's my gunner? Where's my navigator?'

'A mental case,' said Dr Antonio. 'Speaks English, hands covered in spaghetti, asks for his navigator. Without doubt, a mental case. Palgrave, fetch a strait jacket.'

Luckily at that moment Mrs Jones walked out, wondering what had become of Ben. When she saw him lying on the ground, his hands covered in spaghetti, she let out a cry.

'Oh, Ben, dear! Whatever has been going on?'

'Do you know this man?' asked Sister Bridget.

'He's my husband. What's happened to him?'

'He seems to have fainted,' said the sister.

Mr Jones came to a bit more. "Is that you, Martha?" he said faintly. 'Worms,' he gasped. 'Worms in my pocket. It was the shock –'

'Oh my goodness gracious, I should think so, whatever next,' cried his wife. 'Worms in your pockets, how did they come to be there, then?'

'It wasn't worms, it was spaghetti,' said the sister, helping Mr Jones to sit up and fanning him with the strait jacket which Palgrave had just brought. 'Could you fetch a cup of tea, please, Palgrave? How did you come to have your pockets full of spaghetti, Mr Jones?'

'Instant coffee, instant stretcher, instant strait jacket, instant tea,' grumbled Palgrave, stomping off again.

'Spaghetti? Oh, that must have been Mortimer, bless his naughty ways,' said Mrs Jones. 'Last time I left him alone with a bowl of spaghetti for five minutes he packed it all in among my Shetland knitting wool. Arabel's friends kept asking where she got her spaghetti Fair-Isle sweater – *Ben!* Where *is* Mortimer?'

Mr Jones struggled to his feet and drank the cup of tea Palgrave handed to him.

'Mortimer? He was here just now. Have you seen a raven?' he asked Palgrave.

'Raven? Big black bird? I chucked him out the window with a cup of Whizzcaff up his tail feathers,' said Palgrave. 'Doc there told me too.'

'Oh no!' wailed Mrs Jones. 'Dr Plantagenet said a sight of Mortimer was the one thing that might make Arabel feel better.'

She looked beseechingly at the sister. Sister Bridget looked at Palgrave. Palgrave looked at Dr Antonio, who looked at his feet.

'Better go outside and start looking for him and be quick about it,' said the sister.

'Instant coffee, instant stretcher instant strait jacket, instant tea, instant raven,' grumbled Palgrave, and followed the doctor out through the fire door on to the fire escape. It was raining hard and very dark indeed.

Where, all this time, *was* Mortimer?

Outside the windows of Balaclava Ward there was a balcony that ran right round the building. Mortimer, when urged out of the window so rudely, had flown no further than the balcony parapet. There he sat in the dark, thinking gloomy thoughts.

He was tired. It had been a long, exciting day: first of all the roller skating, then the bananas, then the chimney, then the soot, then the two-mile walk from Auntie Brenda's house to Rainwater Crescent. Then the traffic lights.

Mortimer's feet hurt and his tail feathers felt fidgety from the Whizzcaff, he was all sooty and his wings ached where Lindy, Cindy and Mindy had pulled them, and he wanted to go to sleep very badly. What he longed for was the lovely, cosy, shiny white enamel bread bin.

But also he had a feeling that Arabel was somewhere not far off, and he wanted to see her.

Limping a little, muttering and croaking under his breath, he started to sidle along the parapet of the balcony, looking through each window as he came to it.

Just inside the third window there stood a bed which at first looked as if there was nobody in it; the person was so very small, and lying so very flat, and not moving at all.

Mortimer flopped across from the parapet to the windowsill and looked through the glass, his black eyes as bright and sharp as pencil points. 'Kaaaark!' he said.

The person in the bed didn't stir.

Mortimer tapped on the closed window with his beak.

Nobody came to let him in. Sister Bridget was talking quietly to Mr and Mrs Jones at the other end of the ward, a long way off. All the other patients were asleep. Nobody heard Mortimer.

Down below, in the pouring rain, Dr Antonio and Palgrave, equipped with torches and butterfly nets, were hunting for Mortimer in the hospital garden. They weren't finding him.

Mortimer sighed. Then he spread his wings and hoisted himself into the air. He flew along the row of windows tapping each in turn. They were all shut. Fresh air was let into the ward through little round ventilators; they were no use to Mortimer.

When he had been all along one side of the ward and back along the other side, Mortimer flew heavily up on to the roof. Here he found a chimney. He perched on it.

The chimney had a familiar sooty smell. Mortimer stuck his head down inside and listened. Then he sniffed. Then he listened again. Then he tapped with his beak against the chimney pot. Then he came to a quick decision and dived head first down the chimney.

Luckily for Mortimer they had given up using stoves to heat Rumbury Central. Instead they had electric radiators. But the stoves were still there, because no one had time to remove them, and it would make a lot of mess anyway.

In the middle of Balaclava Ward there stood a big blue coal-stove, shiny, with a big black stovepipe leading up from it, and two doors that opened in front. They had shiny little mica panes

so that when they were shut you could see the fire behind them.

Mortimer came clattering down the chimney head first and landed inside the stove, with two pounds of clinker and a handful of soot – though nothing like so much as had been in Auntie Brenda's chimney, because this one had been regularly swept. This surprised him very much; it was not what he had been expecting.

He made the most amazing noise inside the stove. Several of the patients woke up and thought it was Santa Claus.

Sister Bridget came running.

Mortimer was trying to open the doors, but he couldn't. He did push his head out through one of the mica panes, though, and glared at Sister Bridget as she came running towards him.

'Is this your raven?' Sister Bridget asked Mrs Jones.

'Oh good gracious, bless my precious soul, *yes*, however did he get in there, the naughty wretch, I'm sure I don't know. Oh, dear Sister Bridget, do get him out of there quick, please! I'm so anxious about Arabel, she doesn't seem to take notice of *anything*.'

Sister Bridget undid the screw that kept the stove doors shut. When she opened the doors, out

swung Mortimer, with his head still stuck through one of the panes. Sister Bridget grabbed him round the middle. She didn't hurt him, but she held him tight while she worked his head backwards through the hole he had made.

Then she held him up and had a look at him.

'Did you *ever* in all your born days see a bird in such a filthy state?' she said. 'That bird is going to have a bath before he goes anywhere near your daughter Mrs Jones, or my name's not Moira Bridget Hagerty.'

'Oh please be quick, then,' sobbed Mrs Jones. 'I think he's her only hope, I truly do! Oh my goodness, I'm sorry I ever said a word against his pecking munching ways and if Arabel gets better he can undo every bath towel and hearthrug we have in the house!'

Sister Bridget carried Mortimer into a white-tiled room called the Sluice and there she suddenly put him under a jet of warm water and squirted liquid soap at him too. Mortimer let out a squawk and struggled as if he were being barbecued. Sister Bridget took no notice at all. She held him in the jet of water until every speck of soot had run off him. Then she clapped a hairdryer over him which was so powerful that before you could whistle *God Save the Queen* he was bone dry and his feathers were sticking out all round like a dandelion clock.

He was still as black as ever. And by this time he was in a bad temper. When Sister Bridget lifted the dryer off him he sidled towards her as if he would have liked to give her a good peck. But Sister Bridget stood no nonsense, from nurses, doctors, or ravens.

'Behave yourself now!' she said sharply to Mortimer, and she picked him up round his black middle and took him over and put him on Arabel's bedside locker.

'Arabel, dearie,' said Mrs Jones, 'here's Mortimer come to see how you are getting on.'

Arabel didn't answer. She lay very white and quiet with her eyes shut.

Mr Jones gave a gulp and blew his nose.

Mortimer looked at Arabel. He looked at her for a long, long time. He sat still on the polished wooden locker staring at her. Arabel didn't move. Mortimer didn't move either. But two tears ran down, one on either side of his bill.

Then he hopped down on to Arabel's pillow. He hopped close beside her head, and listened at her left ear. He listened for a long time. Then he went round to the other side and listened at her right ear.

Then he croaked a little, gently, to himself, and made a tiny scratching noise with his claws on the pillow. Then he waited.

There was a pause. Then, very slowly, Arabel
rolled over on to her stomach. She turned her face
a little and opened one eye, so that she could just
see Mortimer with it.

'Hullo, Mortimer,' she whispered.

Nobody breathed much.

Then she turned her head the other way, so that
she could see Mrs Jones.

'Mortimer's tired. He wants his bread bin,' she
whispered.

'Oh, Ben – *quick*!' Mrs Jones gulped.

Mr Jones went very quickly and quietly out of
the ward. He didn't like to run until he was on the
other side of the door. Then he fairly hurled himself
down the stairs and rushed out to his taxi.

'Bird's found; going to get bread bin,' he panted as he ran past Palgrave and Dr Antonio, who were standing in the forecourt scratching their heads.

Mr Jones drove home as fast as he dared. He ran into the kitchen at Number Six, Rainwater Crescent. He tipped one farmhouse, one wholemeal, one currant malt and a bag of rice buns on to the floor, and carried the bread bin out to the taxi. He hadn't even switched off the engine.

When he got back to the hospital everyone was in exactly the same position as when he had left, except that Palgrave was there too with a pot of cocoa, and Dr Antonio with a bright scarlet rash.

Arabel had shut her eye again, but when her father whispered, 'Here's the bread bin, dearie,' she opened it.

'Please put it on the bed,' she whispered, and curled herself into a C shape.

Mr Jones put the bread bin into the middle of the C. It had two enamel handles, one on each side. Mortimer stepped down from Arabel's pillow and climbed carefully, by means of one of the handles, on to the rim of the bin. He perched there for a minute, then he jumped down inside. Then he stuck his head under his wing and went to sleep.

Arabel reached out a hand from under the
bedclothes and took hold of the enamel handle.
Then, holding the handle, she too went to sleep.

'Would you credit it, now?' said Sister Bridget.

'Oh my gracious, now I suppose we'll have to
keep the bread in the coal scuttle,' said Mrs Jones.
Mr Jones sat down beside her and they went on
sitting by Arabel all night. In the morning
Dr Plantagenet came to have a look at Arabel.
Her cheeks were just faintly pink, and her eyes
were quite bright. Mortimer was as black as ever,
still fast asleep in his bread bin.

Mortimer's Tie

I

O N A BEAUTIFUL, sunny, warm Saturday halfway through March, something happened in Rainwater Crescent which was to lead to such startling consequences for the Jones family that, even years afterwards, Mrs Jones was liable to come over funny if she so much as heard a piano being played – while the sight of a tin of lavender paint, or any object that had been painted lavender colour, brought her out in severe palpitations. As for Mr Jones, he was often heard to declare that he would let mushrooms grow on the floor of his taxi – or even mustard and cress – before he would permit any person other than himself to clean it out, ever again.

Perhaps it will be best to start at the beginning.

On Saturday afternoons Mr Jones, who was a taxi driver, always allowed himself two hours off to watch football. (In winter that was, of course; in summer he watched cricket.) If Rumbury Wanderers were playing on their home ground – which was just five minutes' walk from the Jones's family house in Rainwater Crescent – Mr Jones went round to cheer his home team; otherwise, he looked at whatever game was being shown on television.

On the Saturday in question he had just returned from a special hire job, taking a passenger to Rumbury Docks. He was late back, so he bolted down his lunch and went off to watch Rumbury play Camden Town.

Mrs Jones was out doing her usual Saturday shopping and having her hair set at Norma's Ninth Wave; otherwise things might have turned out differently. While Mr Jones was taking his time off, Chris Cross, who had just done his A-levels at Rumbury Comprehensive, cleaned out Mr Jones's taxi cab, which was left parked for the purpose in front of the house in Rainwater Crescent.

For doing this job Chris got paid one pound, plus an extra-good high tea. Arabel Jones, who was still too young for school, helped Chris, but she did it for pleasure and did not get paid; however she got a share of the high tea, and had free rides all the time in her father's taxi, so the arrangement seemed fair.

Mortimer, the Jones's family raven, also helped clean the cab; or at least he was present while the job was being done.

Chris set about it as follows: first he carried Mrs Jones's vacuum cleaner (it was the upright kind, and was called a Baby Vampire) out on to the pavement in front of the house, taking its cord through the drawing-room window and across the garden (luckily it was a good long cord); Chris then removed the rubber mats from the floor of the taxi, laid them on the pavement, and washed them; then he vacuumed the inside of the taxi with the Baby Vampire; then he washed the floor with hot water and Swoosh detergent. Next, using the garden hose, he washed the outside of the taxi all over (first making sure the windows were shut). Then he gave the windows and windscreen an extra going-over with Windazz. Then he gave the rest of the outside a polish. Then he put back the floor mats, which had had time to dry by now, and cleaned the inside upholstery with Seatsope. And he finished off by polishing the door and window handles and any other shiny bits on the dashboard with Chromoshino.

Or at least, all that was what Chris intended to do. But Mortimer the raven was taking such an active interest in the proceedings that matters turned out differently.

First Mortimer sat on the vacuum cleaner and had all his tail feathers blown sideways. Also a

green tie, which he happened to be wearing wound several times round his neck, became unwound, and was blown twenty-five yards down the street. Arabel had to go after it; she rolled it up and put it into the glove compartment for safekeeping. Mortimer, slightly irritated by having his tail disarranged, had in the meantime pecked a hole in the bag of the vacuum cleaner, so Chris had to do the rest of the job with the brush and dustpan.

Then Mortimer got tangled up in the hose. During his frantic efforts to disentangle himself he pecked several holes in the hosepipe; after that water came out all over the place.

Next, Mortimer trod on the cake of Seatsope, which Chris had carelessly left on the front doorstep; it skidded away with Mortimer on it and narrowly missed a passing van. So Arabel decided to put Mortimer inside the taxi. Here he perched on the rim of the pail containing hot water and Swoosh. There was not much water left in the pail, which tipped over with Mortimer's weight. Mortimer swiftly removed himself from the floor, where he had been ankle-deep in suds, and clambered on to the steering wheel, where he studied all the dashboard fittings with keen attention.

'It would be a lot easier to get on with the job if that bird stayed indoors,' said Chris, wringing out the bottom of his jeans and giving Mortimer an unfriendly look. Both Arabel and Chris were wet all over by this time, what with one thing and another, while Mortimer was perfectly dry; the water just ran off his thick black feathers.

'Ma doesn't like Mortimer to be left alone indoors,' Arabel said, 'not after the time he ate all the taps off the gas cooker. He didn't *mean* to knock over the bucket. Why don't you switch on the heater – that will dry the floor.'

Chris had the car keys in his jeans pocket. He moved Mortimer off the steering wheel and on to the back seat; then he turned on the ignition; then he switched on the fan heater, which began to blow hot air all over the place.

Mortimer had been watching all this with absorbed interest. He had been thinking a lot about keys, lately; in fact he had started a small collection of them, which he kept in an old money box of Arabel's at the back of the broom cupboard.

Now Mortimer stepped thoughtfully down on to the floor (leaving some toenail holes in the leather upholstery) and began to walk about, enjoying the warm draught on his stomach; he also left dirty bird footprints on the damp floor.

'I wish he'd keep his feet in his pockets,' said Chris.

'He hasn't any pockets,' said Arabel.

Mortimer then returned to the steering wheel in three quick movements – flap, hop, thump – and tweaked out the ignition key with his strong, hairy beak. Next he flopped right out of the taxi through its open front door and made his way quite fast to the pillar box which stood on the pavement outside the Joneses' house. He was just on the point of dropping the car keys through the slot of the letterbox when Chris, leaping from the taxi like a grasshopper, grabbed him round the middle and took back the keys.

'No, you don't, Buster; you just keep your big beak out of what doesn't concern you,' said Chris;

and he dumped Mortimer, none too gently, on the rear seat once more.

Mortimer began to sulk. The way he did this was to sink his head between his shoulders, ruffle up his neck feathers, turn his beak sideways, curl up his claws, and, in general, look as if for two pins he would puncture the tyres or smash the windows.

'He wants to help, really,' said Arabel. 'The trouble is, he doesn't know how. I'll tell you what, Mortimer – why don't you hunt for diamonds behind the back seat?'

Mortimer gave Arabel a very sour look. Actually, until a few days ago, he had been quite keen on searching for diamonds; it had been his favourite hobby and he did it all over the place, specially under carpets, and in coal scuttles and paper and string drawers; but he had found so few diamonds – indeed, none – that he had lately lost interest in this pastime. Instead, he had become interested in keys. He liked the way they fitted into locks, and the different things that happened when the keys were turned – like engines starting, and doors opening. He had developed an interest in letterboxes too.

So he was not pleased at being asked to hunt for diamonds.

However, when Arabel pointed out to him the deep crack between the cushion and the back of the rear seat, he began to poke along it in a grudging manner, as if he were doing her a big favour.

In fact the crack *was* very narrow and inviting; just the right place to find a diamond and his beak was just the right length to go into it nicely. The surprising thing was that almost at once Mortimer *did* find a diamond, quite a big one, the size of a stewed prune. It was set in a platinum ring.

'Kaaaark!' said Mortimer, very amazed. The remark came out slightly muffled, as if Mortimer had a cold, because the platinum ring was jammed over his beak.

'Oh!' said Arabel. 'Chris! Just *look* what Mortimer's found!' She slid the ring off Mortimer's beak; just in time, for otherwise he would certainly have scraped it off with his claw and then swallowed it.

'Coo,' said Chris. 'What a size! That stone is probably worth half Rumbury Town! D'you think we ought to fetch your dad?'

'Pa simply hates to come home before the match is finished,' said Arabel.

Just at that moment they heard the phone inside the house begin to ring. Arabel took the diamond ring from Mortimer, slipped it on her finger and went in through the front door to answer the phone.

Mortimer sidled after her, keeping a sharp eye on the ring. But as he passed the front door he poked a worm, which he had picked up for the purpose, through the letterbox into the basket behind.

The Joneses' telephone stood on the windowsill halfway up the stairs. 'Hello?' said Arabel, picking up the receiver and sitting on the middle step.

'Hello?' said a lady's voice. 'Oh my goodness, can I speak to Mr Jones the taxi driver who drove me to Rumbury Docks this morning? This is Lady Dunnage speaking. Mr Jones took me to launch my hubby's new cruise liner, the *Queen of Bethnal Green* –'

All these words came out very fast and breathless, joined together like the ribbon of paper from a cash register.

'I'm afraid Mr Jones is out just now watching football,' said Arabel. 'This is his daughter speaking.'

'Oh my goodness, then, dear, when will your father be back? The thing is, I've lost my diamond ring which is worth two hundred and seventy thousand, four hundred and twenty-two pounds – I just looked down at my finger and it wasn't there – the ring I mean – the finger is there, of course – and my hubby will be upset when he finds out – specially if it fell into Rumbury Dock.

I just wondered if it could have come off in the taxi when I took my gloves off to unwrap a lemon throat lozenge –'

'Oh yes, that's quite all right, we found it,' said Arabel. 'The ring, I mean.'

'You *have*? You really have? Oh, what a relief! Oh, goodness, I feel quite trembly. I'll come round at once and fetch it as soon as I can – I'm in Bishop's Stortford now, opening a multistorey amusement park –'

'Kaaark,' said Mortimer, who was now sitting on Arabel's shoulder.

'I beg your pardon, dear?'

'Oh, that was our raven, Mortimer. It was Mortimer who found your ring, actually,' said Arabel.

'Really? Fancy,' said Lady Dunnage. 'I've got a parrot called Isabella, and she's ever so clever at finding things. Well, I can tell you, there will be a handsome reward for *everyone* concerned in finding my ring, and please, please don't let it out of your sight until I get there.'

'That was Lady Dunnage, the person who owns the ring,' said Arabel, returning to Chris. 'She's going to call in and pick up the ring as soon as she can get back from Bishop's Stortford, so we shan't need to fetch Pa from the football match.'

'How do you know it was her and not a gang of international jewel thieves?' said Chris.

'I didn't think of that,' said Arabel. 'Do you think we ought to tell the police about it?'

She looked at the huge diamond on her finger, which Mortimer was eyeing too. However, at this moment, Mrs Jones came up the street with a basket full of shopping and a carton of banana-nut-raisin ice cream under her arm, and her hair all smooth and curly and tinted Bohemian Brown.

As soon as she caught sight of the large flashing stone on Arabel's finger, Mrs Jones began to scold. 'How often have I told you not to go to the shops without me, Arabel Jones, you naughty girl, there's mumps about and I told you to stay right here at home till I got back and not leave Mortimer liable to get up to mischief. I declare as soon as I leave the house trouble sets in and spending your pocket money on that cheap trashy jewellery instead of a nice sensible toy or even a book.'

'It's all right, Ma,' said Arabel. 'I didn't spend any pocket money on the ring. Mortimer found it in Pa's taxi and the lady it belongs to, Lady Dunnage, is coming round to fetch it as soon as she can –'

'Lady *Dunnage*?' screeched Mrs Jones. 'And me with the best cushion covers at the laundry, no tea ready, a week's shopping to put away, soapy water all over the front steps and the hose and the Baby Vampire and goodness knows what else out on the pavement –'

However, they all helped put these things away, as well as the bucket, the sponge, the soap, the brush and dustpan, the various rags and bits of towel and tins of Windazz and Chromoshino that Chris had been using.

Even Mortimer carried in the cake of Seatsope, but as he was later found to have dropped it into the kettle, his help was not greatly valued. He sat on the kitchen taps looking melancholy, with one foot on the cold, one on the hot, and his tail dangling into the sink, while Mrs Jones emptied out the kettleful of hot froth and put on some more water to boil in a saucepan.

By the time Lady Dunnage arrived they had tea set out on the table with three kinds of cake, sausages and chips and eggs, sardine salad, a plateful of meringues, a plateful of kreemy kokonut surprises, and masses of biscuits.

Even Mortimer cheered up; although he still felt unappreciated, he loved sausages and chips and meringues. If allowed, he speared the sausages

with his beak, threw the chips into the air before swallowing them, and jumped on the meringues till they collapsed.

Lady Dunnage did not seem in the least like a member of a gang of international jewel thieves. She was quite short, and all dressed in furs, and her hair was just as shiny and curly as Mrs Jones's, but the colour of a lemon sponge. As soon as she was inside the door she cried out: 'Oh, I can see you are all just as good and kind as you can be and just like dear Mr Jones who is my favourite taxi driver and I always ask for him when I ring up the rank and I'm so grateful I hardly know what to say. Words fail me, they really do, for I should never have heard the last of it from my husband Sir Horatio Dunnage if that ring had been lost. It was my engagement ring that he bought for me twenty years ago last January, and which would you rather have, two thousand pounds or a cruise to Spain on the *Queen of Bethnal Green*?'

'I beg your pardon, dear?' said Mrs Jones, quite puzzled, pouring the guest a cup of tea.

'The *Queen of Bethnal Green*, that's my husband's new cruise liner. He's Sir Horatio Dunnage, you know, who owns the Star Line and the Garter Line and now this new Brace and Tackle line. So say the word and you can all come for a ten-day cruise in a first-class suite sailing on Saturday the nineteenth. Now which would you really rather have, that or the two thousand pounds?'

'Oo – I've *always* wanted to go on a cruise!' said Mrs Jones, who could hardly believe her luck. But then she remembered something and said: 'Really it was Mortimer who found the ring, though, wasn't it, Arabel, dearie? I don't know if he'd like a cruise; what do you think?'

'I expect he would,' said Arabel. 'He generally likes new things. Would you like a cruise, do you think, Mortimer?'

Mortimer thought he would. He couldn't reply, for his beak was full of kreemy kokonut surprise, but his eyes sparkled and he began to jump up and down.

'Of course he'd like it, bless him!' said Lady Dunnage. 'My parrot Isabella just loves being on board ship. That's settled, then! I'll get my hubby's secretary to send you a note about embarkation time. I'll be on the cruise myself, as it's the first one, and so will Isabella, and I'm sure she and Mortimer will make great friends.'

'I don't know if Mortimer's ever met a parrot,' said Arabel a little doubtfully. 'But I expect it will be all right.'

Arabel was greatly excited at the thought of a cruise. But Chris, when Lady Dunnage invited him, said he always got seasick on boats, and he would really prefer a little cash to put towards a motorbike for which he was saving up. Lady Dunnage promised that he should have, not the money, but the bike itself the very next day. Then she left them, gazing so happily at her recovered ring that she never even noticed the worm in the front door letterbox.

When Mr Jones came home after the football and heard that they were all going on a cruise to Spain which they had chosen instead of two thousand pounds, he was very put out indeed.

'Going on a *cruise*? To *Spain*? In *March*? Taking *Mortimer*? Instead of two thousand hard cash? You must be stark, staring barmy,' he said. 'Mark my words, no good will come of this.'

He was really annoyed. He threw down his evening paper and Rumbury Wanderers' football scarf and went off to watch television, calling back over his shoulder, 'Anyway, what's that child doing up so late? It's high time she, *and* that bird,

were in bed. Cruise to Spain, indeed. What next, I should like to know?'

After Arabel and Mortimer had gone slowly upstairs, Arabel remembered that Mortimer's green tie had been left outside in the glove compartment of her father's taxi; she had to put on her trousers and duffel coat over her pyjamas and go down again to get it. Mortimer would not have dreamed of going to bed without his green tie.

So, on the Saturday following Mortimer's discovery the Jones family set off on their cruise.

Mr Jones's friend Mr Murray drove them in his taxi to Rumbury Docks. Rain was coming down as if someone had tipped it out of a pail, and an east wind as sharp as a breadknife came slicing along the dock to meet them.

Mortimer was in a bad mood. At that moment he would much rather have been asleep in the bread bin, with his green tie wrapped round and round his neck and his head tucked under his wing, and perhaps a bunch of keys hooked over one of his toenails.

However, when he saw the cruise liner he began to take more interest in the adventure.

The *Queen of Bethnal Green* was all painted white and blue, and sparkling with newness. She had three white spikes sticking up from her top, four rows of portholes, and a very large blue-and-white-striped funnel.

A friendly steward was waiting by the gangway to escort the Jones family to their quarters. By now Mortimer was becoming very interested in everything, but it was raining quite hard, so Arabel picked him up and carried him on board.

Their cabins were up on the top deck, so they went up in a lift, together with their luggage. Mr and Mrs Jones were in a large room with two beds and several armchairs. Arabel and Mortimer were next door; their cabin was smaller, but much nicer, for it had bunks with pink blankets, one above the other, instead of mere beds.

Arabel would have preferred the upper bunk (which was reached by a ladder) but Mortimer climbed into it directly, going up the ladder beak over claw, very fast, and made it quite plain that he was not going to stand for any arguments about their sleeping arrangements.

'We'll be lucky if he hasn't eaten the ladder before the end of the trip,' Mr Jones said, 'seeing how he nibbles the stairs at home.'

'Nevermore,' said Mortimer.

Mr Jones looked out at the rain, which was splashing down on to the deck outside the portholes.

'I'm sure I don't know how you're ever going to keep that bird occupied and out of mischief for ten days, not if the weather's like this. Have you brought anything for him to do?'

'He's got his tie,' said Arabel.

The tie was an old green one that had once belonged to Mr Jones. Just before Christmas Mortimer had found it in a ragbag and had taken a fancy to it. When he was feeling tired, or bad-tempered, or sulky, or sad, or just thoughtful, he

liked to wind the tie round his neck (which he did by taking one end in his beak, and then slowly and deliberately turning round and round); when the tie was all wound up, he would proceed to work his head and beak (still holding the other end of the tie) well in under his left wing, and he would then sit like that for a long time. One rather inconvenient feature of this habit was that Mortimer preferred the tie to be ice-cold when he put it on; if, when he suddenly felt the need for the tie, he found that it had been left lying in the sun or near the fire and felt warm to the touch, he was quite likely to fly into a passion, croaking and flapping and jumping up and down and shouting 'Nevermore' at the top of his lungs.

On account of this, when they were at home, in spite of Mrs Jones's grumbles, Arabel kept the tie in the ice compartment of the refrigerator, so that it was always nice and cold, ready for use. And if they were going on a trip somewhere, in

Mr Jones's taxi or in a train, Arabel trailed the tie out of the window, holding tightly to one end.

Arabel began to worry now about the temperature of the tie. Her cabin was centrally heated – very warm – and the portholes were not the kind that open. 'Do you think there is a fridge on this ship where we could keep the tie?' she asked her father.

'I'll see to it for you,' said the steward, who was just carrying in Arabel's suitcases. 'The lady in the next cabin has a big suite with a kitchenette; I'll put it in her fridge. Then, any time you want it, ring for me, press that red button there over your dressing table, and I'll come along and get it out for you. My name's Mike.'

'Won't the lady mind?' said Arabel.

'Not she. It's Miss Brandy Brown, the lady who's in charge of entertainments on the ship; her and that group they call the Stepney Stepalives. She's hardly ever in her cabin.'

Arabel and Mortimer followed Mike into the corridor and watched him unlock the door next to theirs, tuck the tie into Miss Brandy Brown's refrigerator, and then, after he had locked up again, put the bunch of keys he carried back into the pocket of his white jacket. 'You'll be all right, then,' said Mr Jones. 'After we've unpacked we'll all go along for a cup of tea.' And he went back to his own cabin.

Arabel and Mortimer took stock of their new quarters. As well as the pink-blanketed bunks, they had a desk and dressing table and two armchairs and a whole lot of mirrors. Mortimer discovered that by looking into one mirror which faced another, he could see an endless procession of reflected black ravens going off into the distance, which he enjoyed very much indeed. There was also a large cupboard for their clothes, and a bathroom.

When Mortimer discovered the bathroom he became even more enthusiastic, because it had a shower, and he had never come across one before. He spent about twenty minutes pressing all the knobs and getting terrific spouts of hot and cold water.

After three inches of water had accumulated on the bathroom floor, Arabel began to be afraid that the water might slop over the doorsill into the bedroom.

'I think you'd better come out now, Mortimer,' she said.

Mortimer took no notice.

But then Arabel, happening to glance out of the porthole, saw Rumbury Docks sliding past at a very rapid rate. 'Oh, quick, look, Mortimer!' she said. 'We're moving! We're going down the Thames!'

In fact, now they thought about it, they could feel the boat bouncing a little through the water, and just then the siren gave a tremendously loud blast: *Who-o-o-o-p.* Mortimer nearly jumped out of his feathers at the noise. And when Arabel held him up to look out and see all the London docks rushing past, he wasn't as pleased as she had expected him to be; he suddenly looked rather unhappy as if his breakfast had disagreed with him.

'My goodness we're going fast already; we're simply shooting along,' said Arabel.

'Nevermore,' muttered Mortimer gloomily.

Not long after this, Mr and Mrs Jones put their heads round the door to say that they were going along to the Rumpus Lounge for tea and entertainment by Miss Brandy Brown.

'Come on, Mortimer,' said Arabel. 'I'm sure you'll enjoy that.'

She picked up Mortimer, hugging him tightly, and followed her parents down the long corridor.

The Rumpus Lounge was a huge room, all decorated in brown and pink and gold, with a balcony round it. On the balcony, and underneath it, were small tables and chairs. In the middle of the room was a big bare space, where people were dancing. There was also a grand piano at one side. Outside the windows, the banks of the River Thames were getting further and further away; and the *Queen of Bethnal Green* was rolling and bouncing up and down a good deal more, as she moved into the open sea.

The Jones family sat down at one of the little tables beside the dance floor, and a waiter brought them tea and cakes. Mortimer began to look more cheerful.

A small and very lively lady walked over to the piano. She had hair the colour of a rusty chrysanthemum and pink cheeks and flashing eyes and a dress that was absolutely covered with sequins which looked like brand-new tenpenny pieces. She began to play the piano and sing a song at the same time:

> 'Swinging down to Spain
> Never mind the rain,
> Way, hay yodelay,
> What a happy holiday!
> Just wait till you tell them where you've been
> On the Queen of Bethnal Green!'

Unfortunately, Mortimer soon began to get overexcited while this was going on and to shout,

'Nevermore, *Nevermore*!' at the end of each verse and sometimes in the middle as well. The lady cast some very annoyed glances in their direction, and presently a waiter came to ask if they could please keep their bird a little quieter, as Miss Brandy Brown didn't like being interrupted. She started singing another song:

'Sail bonny boat like a bird in the air,
Over the sea to Spain.
Oh what a riot of fun we'll share,
Out on the bounding main.
Dancing and singing and eating and drinking
Cancel all care and pain,
If we were clever we'd sail on and never
Ever go home again . . .'

Mortimer seemed to disagree strongly with the sentiment of this song, for he muttered, 'Never, never, never, never, never KAAARK,' all the time that Miss Brown was singing it, his voice growing louder and louder, until she suddenly lost patience, left the piano, and strode over to their table.

Keeping their large silver teapot warm was a blue quilted tea cosy; Miss Brown picked this up, and clapped it over Mortimer like a fire extinguisher. Then she walked away, just in time, as Mortimer kicked off the tea cosy in about five seconds flat, and emerged looking very indignant indeed.

Luckily at this moment Lady Dunnage appeared and came up to their table; she was wearing a pink-and-grey silk dress and she carried, perched on a bracelet on her wrist, a grey parrot with a long scarlet tail. Mortimer's eyes almost shot out on stalks when he saw the parrot; he became completely silent and stared with all his might. The parrot stared back. She had a beak that was curved like the back of a spoon, and she looked very knowing indeed.

'I do hope you are enjoying yourselves, dears,' said Lady Dunnage.

'Oh yes, thank you, dear, we're having ever such a nice time,' said Mrs Jones.

'This is my parrot Isabella,' said Lady Dunnage.

'Kaaaark,' said Mortimer.

'I've arranged for you to sit at Captain Mainbrace's table for dinner; he has a son called Henry who is about your age, Arabel. And do let me know if there's anything you want in the meantime.'

'Oh, please,' said Arabel, 'could your parrot come to my cabin and play with Mortimer? I think he'd like that.'

'Certainly,' said Lady Dunnage graciously. 'I'm sure Isabella would enjoy it too. When she wants to come back to me, just let her out into the passage; she knows her way all over this ship, as we came on board such a lot while it was being built.'

'Can she talk?' Arabel asked.

'Not really yet; she's only a year old. All she can say is 'Hard Cheese'.'

Arabel went back to her cabin with a bird perched on each shoulder. In spite of the very good tea, she knew that Mortimer had not been enjoying himself in the Rumpus Lounge; somehow his bright black eyes didn't seem as bright as usual, and he kept swallowing; Arabel was worried in case he wasn't going to be happy on the cruise.

However, once back in the cabin, he seemed to cheer up. Arabel had thought the two birds might like to play with marbles or tiddleywinks, both of which she had brought with her, but they did not; they took it in turns climbing the ladder to the upper bunk and then jumping off on top of one another. Then they took it in turns shutting each other in Arabel's suitcase and bursting out with a loud shriek. Then they had a very enjoyable fight, rolling all over the floor and kicking each other; showers of red, grey and black feathers flew about. Mortimer shouted 'Nevermore!' and Isabella screamed 'Hard Cheese!' Between them they made a lot of noise and presently the door burst open.

There stood Miss Brandy Brown, her eyes flashing even more than the sequins on her dress. '*Will* you stop making such a row? I'm trying to rest,' she said, very crossly indeed.

The instant she opened the door Isabella flew out through it like a feathered bullet, so that all Miss Brandy Brown saw inside the room was Arabel, looking perfectly tidy, and Mortimer, looking decidedly *un*tidy.

'If that bird makes any more disturbance I shall tell Captain Mainbrace that he's got to be shut up in a crate in the hold!' she said. Then she went out, slamming the door, and flounced back to her own cabin. She was not best pleased when, ten minutes later, Mike the steward tapped on the door and came in.

'It's just to fetch the tie, Miss,' he said.

'Tie? What tie?'

'Tie for the young lady's raven next door,' said Mike, taking it from the fridge and tiptoeing out again. After that, relations were rather strained between Mortimer the raven and Miss Brandy Brown.

On the second day at sea, luckily, the weather was calm, if rather foggy. Arabel spent a good deal of time in the Games Room, playing table tennis with Henry Mainbrace, the captain's son. This was fine, so long as they managed to keep a rally going and the ball stayed on the table. But Mortimer and Isabella were watching, perched like umpires on a convenient pile of folding deckchairs. Every time a ball went on to the floor, either Isabella or Mortimer would swoop down and swallow it. By eleven o'clock each bird had swallowed so many balls that Henry declared he could hear them rattling inside.

'All those balls can't be good for them,' Arabel said rather anxiously.

'No worse than having eggs inside you,' Henry pointed out.

At this point Mr Spicer, the steward who was in charge of the Games Room, came in. When he discovered that Mortimer and Isabella between them had swallowed seventeen ping-pong balls he said that was quite enough, and they had better play somewhere else, or there would be none left for the other passengers.

They went and played with the fruit machines for a while, as Mortimer loved putting coins into slots. But nobody won anything, and presently they ran out of cash. Also Mortimer was discovered posting a whole lot of potato crisps into a letterbox labelled 'Suggestions'.

'It's supposed to be for people who have good ideas for entertainments,' said Henry.

'Now your father will think people want more potato crisps,' said Arabel.

'Or not so many,' said Henry. 'Let's go out on to the Promenade Deck.'

'Oughtn't we to put on our raincoats?' said Arabel, who wasn't sure that Mortimer wanted to go outside.

Isabella definitely didn't want to go; she flew off in the direction of Lady Dunnage's cabin.

'It's only fog,' said Henry. 'Fog doesn't wet you.'

Out on the big triangle of deck to the rear of the Games Room, everything looked very misty and mysterious. When Arabel and Henry walked right to the back, they could see the ship's wake, creaming away into the fog like two rows of white knitting. Arabel held tight on to Mortimer's leg, in case he should be tempted to try flying. The ship was going so fast that if he did, she was afraid he might be left behind. But Mortimer displayed no wish to fly; on the contrary. He huddled against Arabel's ear and muttered, 'Hek-hek-hek,' which was his way of informing her that he wanted to put on his tie.

As it happened, Arabel had the tie in her cardigan pocket. She pulled it out and waved it in the cold, damp, foggy air until it was cool enough to satisfy Mortimer. Then she carefully wrapped it round and round him and walked along the deck carrying him wrapped up like a cocoon.

'I'm afraid he's not enjoying the trip very much,' she said.

'He'll like it better when the weather gets hotter,' Henry said.

They had come to a big flat square in the middle of the deck with a handle on it.

'What's that?' said Arabel. 'It looks like the cover of a cheese dish.'

'It is a cover,' Henry said. 'The swimming pool's under there. When the weather gets hot, they lift off that cover with a hoist and we can swim. The water's heated.'

'I hope it gets warmer soon,' said Arabel. 'It isn't very hot now.'

A few people were sitting out in deckchairs, but they were all wrapped up in thick rugs, like Mortimer in his tie.

Mr Spicer came out with a trayful of steaming cups and handed them round to the people in the chairs.

'What's that?' Arabel asked.

'Hot beef tea and cream crackers,' said Henry.

Mortimer sniffed, opened one eye, and poked Arabel's ear to inform her that he wanted to try a cup of hot beef tea. However, when he had tasted a beakful of the stuff he decided that he did not like it, and spat it out, making a very vulgar noise

which caused all the ladies and gentlemen in the deckchairs to raise their eyebrows. He poked the cream cracker in among the folds of his tie.

Arabel and Henry walked on quickly, up some stairs, and along a narrower part of the deck towards the front end of the ship. Mortimer huddled down inside his tie and shut his eyes again.

'What are all those small boats hanging up there in a row?' Arabel asked.

'They're the lifeboats,' Henry told her. 'If the ship is wrecked or someone falls overboard, they unhook the boats and slide them down those sloping things, which are called davits, into the sea.'

'There don't seem to be very many boats; are there enough for all the passengers?' Arabel said.

'Each one holds thirty people and there are fifteen on each side.'

'But how many people are there on the ship?'

That, Henry didn't know.

Near the end of the deck they came to another flight of steps, leading up to a locked door.

'What's in there?' asked Arabel.

'That's the bridge, where they have all the controls and steer the ship,' said Henry. 'It's like the driver's cab of a train.'

Arabel had never been in the driver's cab of a train, so that did not help.

'Well, it's like the dashboard of a car,' said Henry. 'I daresay my dad will let you go in and look at it sometime.'

Just then a dreadful thing happened.

The nearer they got to the forward end of the ship, the harder the wind blew, because the ship was travelling fast, and there was nothing to screen them. It was like standing up in an open car that is rushing along at sixty miles an hour.

When they reached the steps leading up to the bridge, Mortimer opened an eye and looked about him. The first thing he noticed was a letterbox slot in the locked door that said 'Captain'. Before Arabel could stop him, he left her shoulder, scrabbled his way very fast, beak over claw, up the rail of the staircase, and posted his cream cracker, which had been tucked in the folds of his tie, through the letterbox.

Then he began to come down again. But the tie, probably loosened by the removal of the cream cracker, was suddenly dragged off his neck by the fresh wind. Quick as thought, before he could even let out a squawk, or Arabel could grab it, the wind whisked it away, over the deck rail and out of view.

'Oh, my goodness –' cried Arabel in utter dismay.

She and Henry rushed to the rail and looked over; but there was nothing to be seen. The fog was now so thick that they could see only a few yards down the side of the ship.

No tie.

It had taken a moment or two for Mortimer, clinging to the balustrade, to understand what had happened. He felt a draught, an unaccustomed chill round his middle. Then he realised that the reason why he felt so unwrapped was because his tie had disappeared. He let out a long and lamentable squawk. 'Ka-a-a-ark!'

'Oh, Mortimer, I'm *sorry*!' cried Arabel.

Mortimer gave her a look of frightful reproach. It said, plain as words, 'What's the use of your sorrow to me? *That* won't keep me warm. Why didn't you tie the tie in a knot?'

Arabel picked up Mortimer and held him tight. 'I'd better take him back to our cabin,' she said.

Henry kindly promised that he would ask his father to tell all the crew to keep a lookout for Mortimer's tie, just in case it had blown to another part of the ship. 'But I'm afraid it's most likely gone straight into the sea,' he said.

Mortimer glared at him balefully.

Arabel carried Mortimer back to their room, stopping at the ship's shop on the way for a bag of raspberry jelly delights. Usually Mortimer was very fond of these, but at this moment he couldn't have cared less about them. Nor did he want to throw patience cards into the air and stab them with his beak, or any of the other activities that Arabel suggested. He made it plain that he wanted nothing but his tie. He croaked and flapped and moped and sulked and sat hunched in the upper bunk looking miserably down at Arabel, or out through the porthole at the heaving grey sea.

To make matters worse the weather was becoming quite rough. The *Queen of Bethnal Green* began to tip up and down, and roll from side to side. Arabel found, presently, that all the lurching about made her feel rather poorly; and as for Mortimer, he started to look decidedly unlike himself; if a bird of his complexion could be said to look green, then Mortimer looked it.

Arabel began to feel really anxious about him.

At last she pushed the red button to summon Mike the steward.

Mike, when he came, was cheerful and reassuring. He examined Mortimer, who was now sitting on Arabel's bunk with his eyes closed.

'Feeling a bit all-overish, is he? You too? Lots o' the passengers are, just now. It'll be better tomorrow when we get across the Bay. You'd better take a couple of Kwenches – they'll put you right in no time. Here you are.' He brought out of his pocket a couple of large pale-green pills. 'There! Guaranteed to relieve any discomfort or

travel sickness or indisposition due to climatic conditions.'

'Oh, thank you, Mike. You are kind,' said Arabel. She swallowed her pill with a glass of water.

'WARNING,' said Mike, reading from the packet. 'These tablets may cause drowsiness. If affected, be sure not to drive or operate machinery.'

'Well, Mortimer and I aren't likely to be operating any machinery,' said Arabel. 'Unless you count the fruit machines. Mike, do you think this tablet is rather large for Mortimer? After all, he's only a bird. Should we cut it in half? Or even a quarter?'

'Maybe we'd better,' said Mike. He dug into his pocket again, and pulled out a collection of jingling things – keys, bottle openers, corkscrews, tin openers and a penknife. But before he could cut the pill in half with any of these tools, Mortimer, who had been peering at it through half-closed eyes for the last few minutes, suddenly opened his beak very wide indeed and swallowed it down. Then he shut his eyes again.

'Oh, well,' said Mike. 'I daresay he'll be all right. He's swallowed plenty odder things than that, if what I hear is true. It'll probably just give him a good nap.' He gathered up his keys and corkscrews.

Mortimer slightly opened his eyes again and directed a hostile look at Mike's back, which was now turned to him, as the steward drew the curtains across the porthole to shut out the dismal view. Very neatly, and without the slightest noise, Mortimer reached out a claw and hooked up a ring of keys which was dangling half out of Mike's pocket, and tucked it under his wing. Neither Mike nor Arabel observed this.

'I'd have a nap, too, if I was you,' said Mike. 'I'll bring you along some tea and sponge cakes, by and by.'

Arabel thought this was good advice. She curled up in her warm pink blankets and had a nap. Mortimer did too, with the keys tucked safely under his wing.

When Arabel woke next, it was five o'clock.
Mike had come back with the tea and sponge
cakes. He also had a large selection of ties.

'Cap'n Mainbrace was sorry to hear from
young Henry that your bird had lost his comforter.
He took up a collection among the ship's officers.
This here's the result.'

There were ties of every kind – spotted, striped,
wool, satin, wide, narrow, plain and bow. But no
dark-green tie.

'Oh, that's very kind of them,' said Arabel.
'Mortimer's still asleep. I'll show them to him as
soon as he wakes up.'

As a matter of fact she was not too hopeful that
Mortimer would like any of the ties, knowing

how hard he was to please. But there would be no harm in trying.

'Let sleeping birds lie,' said Mike. 'I wouldn't rouse him till he wakes of hisself. I was to tell you that your ma's having her hair done in the Beauty Salon, and your pa's playing bingo.'

Arabel certainly had no intention of rousing Mortimer. She tiptoed away, leaving him still fast asleep, warmly cocooned in pink blankets. And just to be on the safe side, she locked the cabin door.

Arabel watched Mr Jones playing bingo for a while, but she did not find it very interesting, and presently she went off with Henry, who came to tell her that a ship's treasure hunt was being organized and she had been invited to help lay the clues.

They had just begun doing this on the Fiesta Deck when they heard loud screams coming from the direction of the Beauty Salon, which was not far away. Screams always made Arabel anxious if Mortimer was anywhere in the neighbourhood; so often they seemed to have some connection with him. She started off towards the Beauty Salon, and saw Miss Brown running down the stairs with half her hair in curlers and the other half loose and floating behind her.

'What is it?' Arabel asked. But Miss Brown rushed past without answering.

Then Mrs Jones came out of the salon. 'Oh my stars, is that you, Arabel?' she said. 'Why ever haven't you been keeping an eye on Mortimer? He came wandering into the beauty parlour as if he was under the affluence of incohol, gliding along with his eyes tight shut and his toes turned up and his wings stuck straight out before him, just like good Queen MacBess on her way to the Hampton Court *Palais de Danse*. It's my belief he's been magnetized by one of those hypopotanists.'

'Oh dear,' said Arabel, 'I thought he was safe in my cabin, fast asleep.'

'He *was* fast asleep. That's what I mean!'

'Why was everybody screaming?'

'Well, it wasn't everybody, dearie,' said Mrs Jones, 'but only that Miss Brandy Brown who, say what you like, is a very silly historical girl to fly off the handle just because she sees a bird; she says she's got an algebra about birds, or an agony – all he did was give her green towel a tweak –'

'Poor Mortimer,' said Arabel, 'I expect he was looking for his tie in his sleep.'

'And then of course a bottle of setting lotion fell on him and, with the dryer on the floor, blowing, all his feathers turned curly, so he did look rather peculiar –'

'I'd better find him,' said Arabel, and hurried off.

When she got to the Beauty Salon, Mortimer was not to be seen, though there was a fair amount of chaos which suggested that he had spent several minutes in there; some dryers were knocked over and blowing hot air in every direction, taps were running, bottles were broken, green nylon overalls and towels lay all over the place, and there were enough scattered hairpins to build a model of the Eiffel Tower.

Henry joined Arabel and they began methodically hunting through the ship. They were partly helped, partly hindered, by the public address system.

'Will any member of the crew or passengers seeing a large raven who doesn't answer to the name Mortimer and is apparently walking in his sleep and searching for a green tie, please contact Miss Arabel Jones, in Cabin 1 K on the Upper Deck?'

'How can he have got out of your cabin? I thought you locked it?' panted Henry, as they ran along the Promenade Deck, examining all the tarpaulin-covered lifeboats, to see if any of them had been disturbed lately.

'I don't understand it,' said Arabel. 'But I've heard when people are walking in their sleep they can fall off high places without getting hurt. Perhaps they can go through locked doors too.'

She didn't know, of course, that Mortimer had Mike's bunch of passkeys, which would open any door on the ship. Nobody knew this until the *Queen of Bethnal Green* suddenly began sailing in circles.

'Losh sakes! What's come wi' the ship?' exclaimed old Mr Fairbairn, the chief engineer, who had gone off duty and was having a cup of tea in the Rumpus Lounge.

He dashed back to the bridge, where the door was swinging open and the second engineer, Hamish McTavish, with a very red face, was declaring: 'I swear to goodness all I did was turn my back for about thirrrty seconds tae charrt the day's course, and yon black ruffian had the lock picked and was in like a whirrlwind –'

Mr Fairbairn roared over the public address system, 'Wull Miss Arrabel Jones come withoot delay tae the brreedge, whurr her raven Morrtimer is mekking a conseederable nuisance o' himself?'

Arabel and Henry rushed to the bridge, but by the time they arrived Mortimer, in his somnambulistic search for his tie, had evidently decided that it was not there, and had left by way of a ventilator. Just after he did so a series of red and green rockets began to shoot up from the *Queen of Bethnal Green.*

'Och, mairrrcy, he must ha' set off the deestress signals when he was sairrching through yon bank o'sweetches,' exclaimed Hamish McTavish, and began hastily sending out radio messages to cancel the message of the distress signals.

Now a new message sounded over the tannoy. 'Will Miss Arabel Jones please come to the first-class kitchen where her raven Mortimer has destroyed seventy-four pounds of iceberg lettuce?'

But long before Arabel and Henry had got to the kitchen, Mortimer had moved on, leaving a trail of green beans, spinach, Brussels sprouts, angelica, broken plates and irate cooks' assistants.

'Will Miss Arabel Jones please come to the casino where a large black bird is wandering around the pool table in a dazed manner with a sprig of broccoli dangling from his beak?'

But by the time they reached the casino, Mortimer had departed, leaving a scene of torn green baize and snapped cues behind him.

'Will Miss Arabel Jones please come to the Swedish gymnasium – the Finnish sauna – the Spanish bar – the Chinese laundry – the Bank – the Crèche – the Card Room – the Library – the Hospital –'

Mortimer was never there.

To add to the confusion, Isabella the parrot, not wanting to be left out of any excitement, was flying gaily about the ship; several times she was grabbed by people who thought she was a raven and that they would be rewarded for capturing her, but Isabella had a very neat left-beak-uppercut combined with a right-claw-hook which ensured that no one ever held her for long. Her activities added most unfairly to Mortimer's general unpopularity.

At last, Arabel, worn out, was obliged to go to bed without having found him.

'Poor Mortimer,' she said sadly. 'I do hope he's got somewhere comfortable to spend the night.'

About an hour after she had gone to bed, Arabel was roused by screams from the cabin next door.

Miss Brandy Brown had been woken by a sound, and had switched on her bedside light just in time to see Mortimer walk slowly through into her kitchenette; open the fridge, and peer gloomily inside. She was so paralysed with astonishment that she did nothing until he had turned and was halfway across the room again. Then she jumped out of bed yelling, 'Help! Murder! Thieves! Jackdaws! Magpies!'

By the time she had reached the door Mortimer, as usual, had vanished from view. She banged on Arabel's door.

'Have you got that bird in there with you?'

'No,' said Arabel anxiously, opening up. 'I only wish I had.'

'Well, he was here just now. And I warn you,' said Miss Brandy Brown ominously, 'if he pesters me any more, I shall take whatever steps seem proper.'

'I don't see how taking steps will help,' Arabel
said, looking at the steps up to Mortimer's bunk.
'Anyway, Mortimer's usually the one who takes
them.'

But Miss Brown had flounced back to her own
room.

It was a night of terror on board the *Queen of
Bethnal Green*. People burst screaming from their
cabins, they rushed in a panic out of lifts and got
jammed in staircases; rumours flew about the
ship far, far faster than Mortimer ever could have.
'There's a mad raven on board – a blood-sucking

vulture – a giant bat – attacks any green article – beware!'

By next morning, luckily, the ship had got through the Bay of Biscay, the weather had turned sunny and hot, and the coast of Spain came into view.

Mortimer was nowhere to be seen, so everybody could relax, except Arabel, who was more and more worried, terribly afraid that he might have fallen overboard, though she hoped, of course, that he had simply found some green thing that would do instead of his tie, and had curled up with it in a quiet corner for a good long nap.

Another person who wasn't happy was Mike the steward. Miss Brandy Brown had sent for him and given him a terrible ticking-off; she accused him of letting the raven into her cabin when he went in to turn down the bed. 'For how else could he have got the door open?' she said. 'He must have been lurking in my cabin for hours.'

It was no use Mike's protesting he had done no such thing. She wouldn't listen, and he felt very ill-used.

After lunch the *Queen of Bethnal Green* anchored off the coast of Spain. Boats came out from the land; anybody who liked could go ashore in them. Lots of passengers went, including Miss

Brandy Brown, and Mr and Mrs Jones. But Arabel said she would prefer to stay on board.

'Don't you want to see Spain, dearie?' said Mr Jones, who in secret thought it sadly probable that Mortimer had been lost overboard.

'No,' said Arabel. 'I shall go on hunting. And they're going to take the cover off the swimming pool and Henry's father is going to teach Henry and me to swim.' With lighter hearts, feeling that their child could hardly be in better hands, Mr and Mrs Jones went off to look at Spain.

Henry and Arabel watched the cover taken off the pool. At one side of the deck there was a small crane, which was used for hoisting heavy objects on board, and now, with one of the crew winding its handle, the crane leaned forward and tweaked the big lid off the pool. Arabel had a secret hope that perhaps Mortimer would be underneath it, but he wasn't.

However they had a very enjoyable swim with Henry's father. But presently the water in the pool began to tip and slop about a good deal, and the sky turned grey, and Captain Mainbrace, glancing up at it, said: 'Looks like dirty weather coming. It's a good thing that the shore boats are due back.'

He hurried off to check his instruments and Henry and Arabel got dressed, then watched the entertainments staff, who were making ready for an open-air concert to be held on deck that evening. The crane dropped the lid back over the swimming pool, and the Rumpus Lounge grand piano was rolled as far as the doorway leading to the open deck. There, a rope was tied round it, and then the crane hooked its hook into the rope, picked up the piano as easily as if it had been a basket of potatoes, and gently dropped it down right on top of the swimming-pool lid.

While this was happening, some members of the entertainments staff were setting out potted palms and orange trees and blooming roses in tubs, and others were painting a huge piece of hardboard with a beautiful sunset scene.

Arabel and Henry watched for a while and then they went off to hunt for Mortimer in all the places they hadn't tried yet. It was a great pity that they went away when they did for, not five minutes after they had gone below, Mortimer himself came wandering out through the door from the Games Room, where he had been dozing behind a pile of deckchairs.

Just at that moment nobody was around. A pot of lavender-coloured paint had been knocked over, and he walked through a puddle of the stuff, leaving a trail of lavender footprints behind him. He was still fast asleep, due to the powerful action of the green pill Mike had given him. He walked with his wings stretched out in front of him, as if he were feeling his way. When he came to the piano stool he climbed up on to it, and so on to the piano, and then, as if he had expected all along that it would be there waiting for him, stepped inside inside the open lid.

Then he lay down on the strings and went on sleeping.

It was just at this moment that Mike came up on deck. The first thing he noticed was the trail of lavender footprints leading up to the piano. Mike tiptoed up to the piano and looked inside. There was Mortimer, lying on his back on the strings, fast asleep, breathing peacefully, with his feet covered in lavender paint.

Quick as a flash, but very quietly, Mike shut down the piano lid and locked it.

His first intention had been to find Arabel and tell her that her companion was safe. In fact he did start off looking for her. But he did not find her at once (she was in the sauna room, right down at the bottom of the ship). In the meantime, Mike couldn't help thinking to himself, 'Wouldn't it be a lark to leave Mortimer inside the piano till Miss Brandy Brown starts to play in the concert this evening? I bet he'd kick up a rumpus! Maybe that would teach snooty Miss B not to make such a carry-on over things people didn't even do.' He was still very sore from the things Miss Brown had said to him.

The shore boats were coming back, and only just in time. The sky was covered with fat black clouds and the wind was getting up, and so were the waves, and there was a low rumble of thunder every now and then.

Captain Mainbrace sent a message to Miss Brandy Brown that her outdoor concert had better be altered to an indoor one, since he was going to hoist up anchor and take the *Queen of Bethnal Green* out to sea until the storm had blown over, to avoid the danger of being washed against the rocky coast. So Miss Brown in her turn sent a message to the scene-shifters asking them if they would move the things back into the Rumpus Lounge; and, wiping the tea from their mouths they came back on deck. Once more the crane was swung out, the rope was knotted round the grand piano, the hook was lowered and tucked into the rope, and the piano was hoisted up into the air.

But just at that moment several things happened simultaneously. The siren let out a blast – wo-o-o-oop – the *Queen of Bethnal Green* started turning round, moving towards the open sea – and a huge wave which had been rolling along towards the liner, met her head on and caused her to bounce from end to end, like a floating sponge when somebody jumps into the bath.

The grand piano, at the end of its rope, swung violently sideways, like a conker on a string – there it was, a piano in mid-air, everybody staring at it; next minute the rope broke, *kertwang!* and there was the piano flying off as if it had been catapulted.

Mike happened to look out through the Rumpus Lounge window and see the piano land in the water – otherwise this story might have ended differently.

'Ohmygawd! What's that piano doing out there in the sea?' he gasped, and rushed out on deck, where, in the pouring rain, the crane operator was apologizing to Miss Brandy Brown and she was saying that playing on that piano was the next thing to playing on an old sardine can anyway, and she for one didn't care if it floated off to the Canary Islands, and there must be another piano somewhere about the ship.

'B-b-but Miss B-b-b-b-brown! Mortimer the raven's inside that piano!' wailed Mike.

Arabel and Henry, who had heard the siren and felt the ship's violent lurch, and had come dashing up on deck to find out what was happening, arrived just in time to hear Mike say this and Miss Brandy Brown reply: 'Well, if that's so, I hope the perishing piano floats right over to Pernambuco with the blessed bird inside it.'

But, luckily for Mortimer, Mr Fairbairn the chief engineer also happened to be passing just then. Henry grabbed his arm. 'Oh, Mr Fairbairn! Arabel's raven is inside that piano!'

'Och, mairrcy, the puir bairrd – whit unchancy hirdum-dirdum gar'd him loup intae sic an orra

hauld at sic a gillravaging time? Yon corbie's cantrips aye fissell us a'fra yin carfuffle tae anither! Bless us a', whit a clamjamfry!'

But while Mr Fairbairn was grumbling and exclaiming in this manner he was not wasting any time; he had raced along the deck and knocked out the pins that held one of the lifeboats, number sixteen, in position; while he did so, Arabel, Mike and Henry scrambled into it; Mr Fairbairn jumped nimbly after them as the boat slid down from its davits and landed in the sea with a plunge and a bounce. Mike started the boat's engine, which began to go chug-chug-chug in a reliable and comforting manner, and just as well, for, seen from down here, the waves looked as huge and black as a herd of elephants, while the sky was getting darker every minute, the thunder growled, the wind shrieked, and lightning, from time to time, silvered the tips of the wave-crests.

'Where's the piano?' cried Arabel anxiously. 'Can you see it, Mr Fairbairn? Is it still floating?'

It was not easy to keep the piano in view now they were down at its level. But back on the *Queen of Bethnal Green* Hamish McTavish had told Captain Mainbrace what was going on, and he helped them by having rockets fired in the direction of the black floating object – it now looked no larger than a matchbox – which was all that could be seen of Mortimer and Miss Brandy Brown's Broadwood. But at last they caught up with the piano. None too soon; it was settling lower and lower in the water as they overhauled it.

'Suppose the water's got inside?' said Arabel.

'Ne' er fash yersel', lassie – I'm after hearing that yon Broad wood craftsmen do a grand watertight job o' cabinetmaking.'

The lifeboat was equipped with a hook, for getting people out of the water, so while Mr Fairbairn steered, Henry hung over the side and managed to hook the piano by the leg, while Arabel clung like grim death on to Henry's feet, and Mike leaned over until he was nearly cut in half by the edge of the boat and, with frightful difficulty, unlocked the lid of the piano.

'Is Mortimer there?' asked Arabel faintly, who could see nothing as she was lying flat holding on to Henry's feet.

'He's there all right,' said Mike, who had almost fractured his spine hoisting up Mortimer's very considerable weight from the sinking piano into the safety of the boat.

'Is – is – is he alive?'

'I reckon he's unconscious,' Mike said. 'We'd better give him a slug of brandy.'

Mortimer lay flat on the bottom boards with his eyes shut and his lavender-coloured feet sticking straight out; from underneath his wing fell Mike's key ring.

'So he's the pilfering so-and-so that half-inched my keys,' said Mike. 'I might have guessed it. Getting me into all that trouble!'

But then he thought how easily Mortimer might have drowned due to his own reckless practical joke, and he knelt down by the motionless raven with the brandy flask from the lifeboat's first-aid box. Just at that moment Mortimer, lying on his back, gave a loud, unmistakable snore. Even over the sound of the engine and the storm they heard it.

'Och, havers, will ye credit it,' said Mr Fairbairn. 'The sackless sumph is still sleeping. Let's gang oor ways back to the ship afore he wakes up.'

It took them much longer to get back to the ship, for all the time they had been rescuing Mortimer the *Queen of Bethnal Green* had been steaming full speed ahead for the open sea, since she did not dare stay close to the dangerous cliffs.

Mr and Mrs Jones had just got back on board when all this excitement began, and had been horrified to see the line of lavender-coloured footprints leading along the deck to nowhere, and to learn that their only child was out in a tiny boat on that black and wicked sea on such a perilous quest. In fact Mrs Jones fainted dead away.

By the time she had come to, the lifeboat had been hauled back on board. Mrs Jones clung to Arabel and hugged her and shook her and slapped her, and laughed and cried and said that Arabel must promise never, *never* to go off again in a boat like that in the middle of such a storm.

'But I'd have to, Ma, if Mortimer was floating away to sea in a piano.'

'I don't care! You shouldn't have gone, even if he was inside a harpsicola! Now go and have a

hot bath this minute, and take that dratted bird with you!'

Luckily, all through this, Mortimer went on sleeping. Arabel had a hot shower, and Mike brought her a delicious supper on a tray, and a whole lot of people came to congratulate her on the brave rescue, and on having Mortimer back safe and sound. All the previous events were forgiven and forgotten; Arabel, Mortimer, Henry, Mike and Mr Fairbairn were the most popular people on the ship. And all this time Mortimer went on sleeping.

Then the best thing of all happened.

Mr Fairbairn arrived carrying a soggy, wet, nasty, messy, salty, sodden, bedraggled bit of dark-green woolly material.

'Hoo are ye the noo, lassie?' he said. 'No' the waur for yer boatie-trip? When I was mekking a' siccar wi' the lifeboat I fund yon clout, an' I bricht it along tae speer is't yon birdie's neck-rag, that a' the blether's bin aboot?'

'Oh, Mr Fairbairn, it *is*! It's Mortimer's tie!' cried Arabel joyfully. 'Oh, thank you, thank you! It must have blown *up*, not down, and got tangled in the davits! Oh, Mortimer *will* be pleased. It's lovely and wet and cold too – just the way he likes it.'

At this moment Mortimer opened one eye. The first thing it saw was his dirty, soggy, wet, bedraggled, salt-encrusted, beloved green necktie.

Mortimer gave a huge sigh of relief, which made his feathers all stick sideways like the petals of a French marigold. (They looked rather like petals too, for they were all curly with setting lotion and salt water.)

Arabel laid the end of the tie by Mortimer's beak, and he took hold of it with a sudden quick snap. Then, shutting his eyes again, he stood up and turned round and round half a dozen times, until he was nicely wound up. Then he dug his head under his wing, lay down, and went back to sleep.

But Mr Fairbairn gave a party, and Arabel and Henry and Isabella went to it, and stayed up till all hours.

The last seven days of the cruise passed quickly. The weather was fine. Miss Brandy Brown played her concert with the Stepney Stepalives, and Arabel and Henry played a lot more table tennis. The *Queen of Bethnal Green* steamed back across the Bay of Biscay, up the English Channel, round the corner of Kent and along the Thames. All this time, Mortimer stayed asleep. Just occasionally, he would open one eye. If it could see water going past outside the porthole, he shut it again.

Then at last, when he opened his eye, he saw the streets of Tilbury going past through Mr Jones's taxi window.

'Kaaaark!' said Mortimer. He opened both his eyes. The streets were still there – beautiful grey rainy streets with houses and shops and traffic lights – no sea anywhere. Mortimer sat bolt upright on Arabel's lap. His black eyes began to sparkle.

'He's *so* glad to be home again,' said Arabel.

'Didn't I say that going on a cruise to Spain would be a horrible mistake? Didn't I?' said Mr Jones. He was driving his own taxi, which Mr Murphy had kindly brought to the dock for him.

Just as they rolled to a stop in front of Number Six, Rainwater Crescent, Mortimer clambered on to the back of the front seat. He reached over Mr Jones's shoulder and pulled the key out of the ignition. Then he flopped out through the taxi door (which Arabel had just opened) and made his way quite fast along the pavement.

'Stop him, *stop him*!' said Mr Jones. 'That bunch has the front-door key on it too.'

But before Arabel could get to him, Mortimer had reached up, tip-claw, and posted the whole bunch of keys into the open slot of the letterbox that stood in front of Number Six.

Then he happily climbed up the front steps, dragging his tie behind him.

The Spiral Stair

'EXCUSE ME. ARE you two gentlemen going as far as Foxwell?' Mrs Jones enquired nervously, having opened the railway carriage door and poked her head through. The hand that was not holding the door handle clasped the wrist of Mrs Jones's daughter Arabel, who was carrying a large canvas bag.

Mrs Jones had been opening doors and asking this question all the way along the train, when she thought the occupants of the carriage looked respectable. Some of them did not. Some weren't going as far as Foxwell.

But the two men in this carriage looked *very* respectable. Both had bowler hats. One was small and stout, one was large and pale. Their briefcases were in the rack, and they were talking to one another in low, confidential, businesslike voices.

Now they stopped and looked at Mrs Jones as if they were rather put out at being interrupted. But one of them – the small fat one – said: 'Yes, madam. We are getting out *at* Foxwell, as it happens.'

The other man, the large pale one, frowned, as if he wished his friend had not been so helpful.

'Oh, are you, that's ever such a relief, then,' cried Mrs Jones, 'for you look like nice reliable gentlemen and I'm sure you won't mind seeing that my little girl, that's Arabel here, gets out at Foxwell where her Uncle Urk will be meeting her and I know it looks ever so peculiar my not going with her myself, but I have to hurry back to Rumbury Hospital where my hubby, Mr Jones, is having his various veins seen to and he likes me to visit him all the visiting hours and I couldn't leave poor little Arabel alone at home every day, let alone Mortimer, and my sister Brenda isn't a *bit* keen to have them, but luckily my hubby's brother Urk lives in the country and said he would oblige, leastways it was his wife, Effie, that wrote but Ben said Urk would know how to manage Mortimer on account of him being used to all kinds of wild –'

Luckily at this moment the guard blew a shrill
blast on his whistle, for the two men were
beginning to look even more impatient, so Mrs
Jones hastily bundled Arabel into the railway
carriage and dumped her suitcase on the seat
beside her.

'Now you'll be ever such a good girl won't you
dearie, and Mortimer too if he *can*, and take care

among all those megadilloes and jumbos and do what Aunt Effie says – and we'll be down to fetch you on Friday fortnight –'

Here the guard interrupted Mrs Jones again by slamming the carriage door, so Mrs Jones blew kisses through the window as the train pulled away. One of the bowler-hatted men – the short fat one – got up and put Arabel's case in the rack where she couldn't reach it to get out her picture book. He would have done the same with the canvas bag she was carrying, but she clutched that tightly on her lap, so he sat down again.

The two men then took their hats off, laid them on the seat, settled themselves comfortably, and went on with their conversation, taking no notice whatever of Arabel, who was very small and fair-haired, and who sat very quietly in her corner.

After a minute or two she opened the canvas bag, out of which clambered a very large untidy black bird – almost as big as Arabel herself – who first put himself to rights with his beak, then stood tip-claw on Arabel's lap and stared out of the window at the suburbs of London rushing past.

He had never been in a train before, and was so astonished at what he saw that he exclaimed '*Nevermore!*' in a loud, hoarse, rasping voice

which had the effect of spinning round the heads of the two men as if they had been jerked by wires. They both stared very hard at Arabel and her pet.

'What kind of a bird is that?' asked one of them, the large pale one.

'He's a raven,' said Arabel, 'and his name's Mortimer.'

'Oh!' said the pale man, losing interest. 'Quite a *common* bird.'

'Mortimer's not a bit common,' said Arabel, offended.

'Well, I hope he behaves himself on this train,' said the pale man, and then the two men went back to their conversation.

Mortimer, meanwhile, looked up and saw Arabel's suitcase in the rack above his head. Immediately he saw it he wanted to get up there too. But Arabel could not reach the rack, and Mortimer was not prepared to fly up. He disliked flying, and very rarely did so, if he could find somebody to lift him. He now said 'Kaark,' in a loud, frustrated tone.

'Excuse me,' said Arabel very politely to the two men, 'could you please put my raven up in the rack?'

This time, both men looked decidedly irritable at being interrupted.

'Certainly not,' said the large pale one.

'Rack ain't the place for birds,' said the short fat one. 'No knowing *what* he might not get up to there.'

'By rights he ought to be in the guard's van,' said the first. 'Any more bother from you and we'll call the guard to take him away.'

They both stared hard and angrily at Arabel and Mortimer, and then began talking to one another again.

'We'd better hire a truck in Ditchingham – Fred will be there with the supplies, he can do it – have the truck waiting at Bradpole crossroads – you carry the tranquillizers, I'll have the nets – twenty ampoules ought to be enough, and a hundred yards of netting –'

'Don't forget the foam rubber –'

'Nevermore,' grumbled Mortimer to himself, very annoyed at not getting what he wanted immediately he wanted it.

'Look at the sheep and the dear little lambs in that field, Mortimer,' said Arabel, for the train had now left London and was running through green country. But Mortimer was not in the least interested in dear little lambs. While Arabel was watching them, he very quietly and neatly hacked one of the men's bowler hats into three pieces with his huge beak, and then swallowed the bits in three gulps. Neither of the men noticed what he had done. They were deep in plans.

'*You* take care of the ostriches – mind, they kick – and *I'll* look after the zebras.'

'They kick too.'

'Just have to be nippy with the tranquillizer, that's all.'

Mortimer, coming to the conclusion that nobody was going to help him, hoisted himself up into the rack with one strong shove-off and two flaps. The men were so absorbed in their plans that they did not notice this either.

'Here's a map of the area – the truck had better park here – by the ostrich enclosure –'

Mortimer, up above them, suddenly did his celebrated imitation of the sound of a milk float rattling along a cobbled street. 'Clinketty-clang, clang, clink, clanketty clank.'

Both men glanced about them in a puzzled manner.

'Funny,' said the short fat man, 'could have sworn I heard a milk cart.'

'Don't be daft,' said the large pale one. 'How could you hear a *milk cart* in a *train*? Now – we have to think how to get rid of the watchman –'

Mortimer now silently worked his way along the rack until he was over the men's heads. He wanted to have a look at their luggage. From one of the two flat black cases there stuck out a small thread of white down. Mortimer took a quiet pull at this. Out came a straggly piece of ostrich feather. Mortimer studied the bit of plume for a long time, sniffed at it, listened to it, and finally poked it under his wing. Presently, forgetting about it, he hung upside down from the rack, swaying to and fro with the motion of the train, and breathing deeply with pleasure.

'Please take care, Mortimer,' said Arabel softly.

Mortimer gave her a very carefree look. Then, showing off, he let go with one claw. However, at that moment, the train went over a set of points – kerblunk – and Mortimer's hold became detached. He fell, heavily.

By great good luck Arabel, who was anxiously watching, saw Mortimer let go, and so she was able, holding wide the two handles of the canvas bag, to catch him – he went into the bag head first.

The ostrich plume drifted to the floor.

The two men, busy with their plans, noticed nothing of this.

The fat one was saying, 'The giraffes are the most important. Reckon we should pack them in first, they take up most room?'

'Nah, can't. Giraffes have to be *un*loaded first. They're wanted by a customer in Working.'

'Why the blazes should somebody want *giraffes* in *Working*?'

'How should *I* know? Not our business, anyway.'

Mortimer poked his head out of the canvas bag. He was very annoyed at his mortifying fall, and ready to make trouble, if possible. His eye lit on the second bowler hat.

Fortunately at this moment the train began to slow down.

'Nearly at Foxwell now, little girl,' said the fat man. He took down Arabel's case and put it by her on the seat.

'You being met here?' he said.

'Yes,' said Arabel. 'My Uncle Urk is meeting me. He is –' But the two men weren't paying any attention to her. The large one was looking for his hat. 'Funny, I put it just here. Where the devil can it have got to?'

'Oh dear,' said Arabel politely, when no hat could be found. 'I'm afraid my raven may have eaten it. He *does* eat things sometimes.'

'Rubbish,' said the hatless man.

'Don't be silly,' said the fat man.

Now the train came to a stop, and Arabel, through the window, saw her Uncle Urk on the platform. She waved to him and he came and opened the door.

'There you are, then,' he said. 'Enjoy your trip? This all your luggage?'

Uncle Urk was brown and wrinkled, with a lot of bristly grey hair. There were bits of straw clinging to his clothes.

'Yes, thank you, Uncle Urk.'

'That's right.' He took Arabel's case, and she carried the bag with Mortimer in it. 'Goodbye,' she called to the two men, but they were still busy hunting for the lost hat.

'Look at this!' the pale one said angrily to the thin one, finding the bit of ostrich plume on the floor. 'You careless fool!' He quickly picked up the feather and stuck it in his pocket.

Uncle Urk dropped Arabel's case in the back of his pickup truck and settled her and Mortimer in the front seat.

'Well? You excited at the thought of staying in a zoo?' he enquired.

'Yes, thank you,' said Arabel. 'Mortimer is too, aren't you, Mortimer?'

'Kaaark,' said Mortimer.

'Do you keep *every* kind of animal in your zoo, Uncle Urk?' Arabel asked.

'It ain't my zoo really, Arabel, you know. I'm just the head warden, and your Aunt Effie runs the cafeteria,' said Uncle Urk. 'The zoo belongs to Lord Donisthorpe.'

'Does he have lions and tigers?'

'No, he hasn't got any of those. He likes grass-eating animals mostly – wildebeests and zebras and giraffes. And birds and snakes. And he's got porcupines and a hippopotamus and a baby elephant. I expect you'll enjoy giving the baby elephant doughnuts.'

'I thought they liked buns best?' said Arabel.

'Lord Donisthorpe has invented a doughnut-making machine,' said her uncle. 'It uses wholewheat flour and sunflower oil and honey, so the doughnuts it makes are very good for the animals. And so they blooming well oughter be at thirty pence apiece,' he muttered to himself. 'Cor! Did you ever? Six bob for a perishing doughnut!'

His truck at that moment passed between gates in a high wire-mesh fence. Arabel noticed a sign that said, 'Caution, zebra crossing'.

Ahead of them lay a ruined-looking castle, inside a moat, and a lot of wooden and stone buildings and haystacks. But Uncle Urk pulled up in front of a small white house with a neat garden round it. 'Here's your Aunt Effie and Chris Cross,' he said.

Chris was a boy who used to live next door to Arabel's family in Rumbury Town, London. But he had come down to work in Lord Donisthorpe's zoo as a holiday job last summer, and liked it so much that he stayed on.

Aunt Effie was thin-faced and fuzzy-haired; her eyes were pale blue but sharp. Nearly all her remarks about people began with the words, 'You can't blame them –' which really meant that she *did* blame them, very much. 'You can't blame the kids who drop their ice-lolly papers; they've never learned no better, nasty little things. You can't blame murderers, it's their nature; what I say is, they ought to make them into pet food. You can't blame your Uncle Urk for being such a muddler, he was born that way.'

Now Aunt Effie's pale-blue eyes snapped as she looked at Mortimer clambering out of his canvas bag, and she said, 'Well, I s'pose you can't blame Martha for sending that monster down with Arabel. *I* wouldn't leave him alone in the house myself, wouldn't keep him a day, but so long as he stays in *my* house, he stops inside the meat safe, that's the place for him!'

She fetched a galvanized zinc cupboard with a perforated door into the front hall and said to Arabel, 'Put the bird in there!'

'Oh, *please* not, Aunt Effie,' said Arabel, horrified. 'Mortimer would hate that, he really would! He's used to being out. I'll keep an eye on him, I promise.'

'Well: the very first thing he pokes or breaks with that great beak of his,' said Aunt Effie, 'into the meat safe he goes!'

Mortimer looked very subdued. He sat beside Arabel at tea, keeping quite quiet, but Arabel managed to cheer him up by slipping pieces of Aunt Effie's lardy cake to him. It was very delicious – chewy and crunchy, with pieces of buttery toffee-like sugar in among the dough, and a lot of currants.

After tea, Aunt Effie had to go back to manage the cafeteria. Chris said, 'I'm going to feed the giraffes, so I'll show Arabel over the zoo a bit, shall I?'

'Mind she's not a nuisance,' said Aunt Effie.

Uncle Urk, who was also going to feed animals, said he would probably meet them near the camel house.

Lord Donisthorpe's zoo was in the large park which lay all round his castle. Lord Donisthorpe lived in the castle, which was in bad repair. The animals mostly lived in the open air, roaming about eating the grass. They had wooden huts and stone houses for cold weather, or to sleep in. Builders were putting up more of these. They were also at work building an enormously high stone wall to replace the wire-mesh fence round the park.

'Is that to stop the animals escaping?' asked Arabel.

'No, they don't want to escape. They like it here,' said Chris. 'It's to stop thieves getting in. There have been a lot of robberies from zoos lately. When this one was smaller, Lord Donisthorpe just used to leave Noah the boa loose at night, and he took care of any thieves that got in. But now the zoo's getting so big there's too much ground to cover – Noah can't be everywhere at once.'

Just at that moment Mortimer's eye was attracted by a beautiful stretch of smooth wet cement which the builders had just laid. It was going to be the floor of the new porcupine palace. Quick as lightning Mortimer flopped off Arabel's shoulder and walked across the cement, leaving a trail of deeply indented bird prints.

'Gerroff there, you black buzzard!' shouted a workman, and he threw a trowel at Mortimer, who, startled, flew up into the nearest dark hole he could find. This happened to be the mouth of the cement mixer, which was turning round and round.

'Oh, please, quick, stop the mixer!' cried Arabel. 'Please get him out!'

A confused sight of feet and tail-feathers could be seen sticking out of the mixer. The man who was running it stopped the engine that turned the hopper, and tipped it so that it pointed downwards. Out came a great slop of half-mixed cement, and Mortimer, so coated over that nothing could be seen of him but his feet and black feathery trousers.

'We'd best pour a bucket of water over him before it sets,' said Chris, and did so. 'Lucky your Aunt Effie wasn't around when *that*

happened,' he added, as Mortimer, croaking and gasping, reappeared from under the cement. 'That'd be *quite* enough to get him shut up in the meat safe.'

'Mortimer, you *must* be *careful* here,' said Arabel anxiously.

Mortimer might have been put out by his mishap with the cement mixer – things like that often made him very bad-tempered – but luckily his attention was distracted just then by the sight of a herd of zebra, all black-and-white stripes.

'Nevermore!' he said, utterly amazed, staring with all his might as the zebras strolled across the road.

Then they passed a group of ostriches, who looked very vague and absent-minded, as ostriches do, and were preening themselves in a patch of sand. When he was close by them, Mortimer did his celebrated imitation of an ambulance rushing past with bell clanging and siren wailing.

All the ostriches immediately stuck their heads in the sand.

'You better tell Mortimer not to make that noise in your Aunt Effie's house,' said Chris. 'Your Aunt Effie doesn't like noise.'

Now they passed a cage which had an enormous, sleepy-looking, greedy-looking snake inside it. 'That's Noah the boa,' said Chris. 'He's very fond of doughnuts. Want to give him one?'

Arabel did not much care for the look of Noah the boa, but she did want to see how the doughnut machine worked. There was one near Noah's cage. It had a glass panel in front, and a slot for putting in a tenpenny piece.

'The public have to put in three coins to get a doughnut,' said Chris, 'but luckily there's a lever behind that only zoo staff know about, so we can get ours for one. You have to put in one tenpenny piece to get it started; after that you keep pulling the lever.'

He dropped a coin in the slot. Instantly an uncooked doughnut rolled down a chute into a pan of boiling oil behind the glass panel, and began to fry. After a minute or two, a wire hook fished it out of the oil and held it up to dry.

'Now, if you were a member of the public, you'd have to put in another coin to get it sugared,' said Chris. 'But as we're zoo staff we can pull the lever.' He did so, and a puffer blew a cloud of honey crystals all over the doughnut so that it became fuzzed with white.

'Now what happens?' said Arabel.

'Now if you were a member of the public you'd have to put in a third coin to get it out,' said Chris. He pulled the lever again. The hook let go of the doughnut, which rolled down another chute and was delivered into a crinkled paper cupcake case.

Mortimer, who had been watching all this with extreme interest, took a step forward along Arabel's arm. But Noah the boa had also been watching – at the first clank of the coin in the machine all his sleepiness had left him – and as Arabel took the doughnut from the paper cup he opened his mouth so wide that his jaws were in a straight line up and down. Arabel rather timidly tossed in the doughnut, and Noah's jaws shut with a snap.

'His jaws are hinged so that he can swallow an animal as big as a pig if he wants to,' said Chris. 'But he prefers doughnuts; they are his favourite food.'

'How do you know?' said Arabel. 'He doesn't *look* pleased.'

'Things he doesn't like he spits out,' said Chris.

'Kaaark,' said Mortimer, in a gloomy aggrieved tone.

'All right, Mortimer,' said Arabel. 'Ma gave me a ten-p piece, so I'll do a doughnut for you now, if Chris doesn't mind pulling the levers.'

She dropped in her coin, and another raw doughnut slid into the boiling oil.

Mortimer's eyes shone at the sight, and he began to jump up and down on Arabel's shoulder.

When the doughnut was cooked and sugared, Chris pulled the lever to release it into the paper cup.

'Suppose a person only had two ten-p pieces?' said Arabel.

'Then they better not start, or they'd have to go off and leave the doughnut waiting there for the next customer,' said Chris. 'But that doesn't often happen. Who'd be such a mug as to leave twenty-p's worth of doughnut for someone else to pick up for only ten-p?'

Just as Mortimer's doughnut came out, something unfortunate happened. A small head on a very long spotted neck came gently over Arabel's shoulder and nibbled up the doughnut so fast and neatly and quietly that for a moment Mortimer could not believe that it had gone. Then he let out a fearful wail of dismay.

'Nevermore!'

'Oh dear,' said Chris. 'That's Derek. These giraffes are just mad about doughnuts. If they see anybody near the machine they come crowding round.'

Arabel turned, and sure enough, three giraffes had come silently up behind them, and were standing in a ring, evidently hoping that more doughnuts were going to be served.

'Their names are Wendy, Elsie and Derek,' Chris said.

'I'm *dreadfully* sorry, Mortimer,' Arabel said. 'I haven't any more money.'

Neither had Chris.

Mortimer made not the least attempt to conceal his disappointment and indignation. He jumped up and down, he screamed terrible words at the giraffes, who looked at him calmly and affably.

'What the dickens is the matter with that bird?' asked Uncle Urk, passing by with a bucket of wildebeest food.

'Derek ate his doughnut,' said Chris.

'Well, for the land's sake, give him another,'
said Uncle Urk, who was very good-natured.
'Here's ten-p.'

'Oh, thank you, Uncle Urk,' said Arabel. This
time she pulled the levers, for Chris had to get on
with his evening jobs.

When the doughnut came down the chute,
Mortimer, who had been watching like a sprinter
waiting for the tape to go down, lunged in and
grabbed it just before Wendy could bend her long
neck down.

He was so pleased with himself at having got in ahead of Wendy that, contrary to his usual habit, he rose up in the air, holding the doughnut in his beak, and flew vengefully and provokingly round and round the high heads of the giraffes.

'Mortimer, stop it! That isn't kind,' said Arabel. 'Just eat your doughnut and don't tease.'

Mortimer took no notice. He swooped between Derek and Wendy, who banged their heads together as they both tried to snatch the doughnut. This amused Mortimer so much that by mistake he let go of the doughnut – which fell to the ground and was seized and swallowed by Elsie.

Mortimer drew a great breath of fury; all his feathers puffed out like a fancy chrysanthemum.

However, Arabel grabbed him and said: 'That just serves you right, Mortimer. I haven't any more money, so you'll have to go without a doughnut now. Come along, we'd better go and see some more of Uncle Urk's zoo.'

She walked on, but Mortimer was very displeased indeed, and kept looking back at the giraffes and muttering, 'Nevermore, nevermore, nevermore,' under his breath.

Then they met Lord Donisthorpe, the owner of the zoo. He was a tall, straggly man, who looked not unlike his own giraffes and ostriches, except that he was not spotty, and had no tail feathers. He had a very long neck, and untidy white hair, and a vague expression.

'Ah, yes,' he said, observing Arabel over the tops of his glasses, which were shaped like segments of orange. 'You must be Mr Jones's niece, come to stay. I hope you are enjoying your visit. But your raven seems out of spirits.'

This was an understatement. Mortimer was now shrieking 'Nevermore!' at the top of his lungs, and spinning himself round and round on one leg.

'One of the giraffes ate his doughnut,' Arabel explained.

'Perhaps he would like an ice cream in the cafeteria?' enquired Lord Donisthorpe. 'Perhaps you would too? They are very good. We make our own.'

'Thank you, we should both like that very much,' said Arabel politely.

On the way to the cafeteria they passed an immensely tall building made of wood and glass. 'That is my new giraffe house,' said Lord Donisthorpe.

At the word *giraffe* Mortimer looked ready to bash anyone who came near him.

The giraffe house was built to suit the shapes of the giraffes, with high windows, so that they could see out, and a spiral staircase in the middle, leading to a circular gallery, so that visitors could climb up and be on a level with the giraffes' faces. The walls of the building were not finished yet; one side was open. Mortimer looked very sharply at the spiral stair, and Arabel kept a firm hold of his leg, for he had been known to eat stairs on several occasions in the past. However these stairs were made of ornamental ironwork, and it seemed likely that even Mortimer would find them tough.

'Come on, Mortimer, Lord Donisthorpe's going to buy you an ice cream,' Arabel said.

'Kaaark,' said Mortimer doubtfully.

The cafeteria, just beyond the giraffe house, had another doughnut machine by its door. Mortimer stared at this very hard as they walked by, but Lord Donisthorpe led the way into the cafeteria itself, which had red tables and shiny metal chairs and a counter with orange and lemon and coffee machines and piles of things to eat. Aunt Effie was at the counter, standing behind a glass case filled with cream-cheese patties and toffee-covered carrots on sticks.

'We make our own toffee-carrots,' said Lord Donisthorpe. 'They are very wholesome indeed. And we have three different flavours of home-made ice cream, dandelion, blackcurrant and quince. Which would you prefer?'

Arabel chose the quince, which was a beautiful orange-red colour; Mortimer indicated that he would like the dandelion, which was bright yellow.

Aunt Effie gave them a disapproving look. '*I* don't know; eating again, only half an hour after they had their tea,' she muttered, scooping out the ice cream and ramming it into cornets. 'But I s'pose you can't blame them, brought up by that empty-headed Martha.'

While she was serving out the ice cream, Mortimer noticed that an empty tray had been left at one end of the cafeteria rail.

Flopping off Arabel's shoulder on to the tray he gave himself a powerful push-off with his tail and shot along the rail past the counter as if he had been on a toboggan, shouting 'Nevermore!' and spreading his wings out wide. His left-hand wing knocked a whole row of cream-cheese patties into the blackcurrant ice-cream bin.

Aunt Effie let out a shriek of rage. 'How Martha can stand that Fiend of a bird in her house I do not know!' she said. 'Ben did warn

Urk that he was a real menace, into every kind of mischief, and I can see he didn't exaggerate. Six patties and seventy-five-p's worth of black-currant ice! You take him straight back to the house, Arabel Jones, and put him in the meat safe, and there he stays, till Ben and Martha come to fetch you.'

The various customers sitting at the little red plastic tables were greatly interested in all this excitement, and many heads turned to look at Mortimer, who had ended up jammed head first in the knife-and-fork rack at the end of the counter, and was now yelling loudly to be released.

Luckily it turned out that Lord Donisthorpe was very fond of cream-cheese patties with blackcurrant ice cream.

'Here,' he said, handing Arabel the red and yellow ice-cream cones, which he had been holding. 'You take these while I find some more money. There you are, Mrs Jones, this will pay for the damaged patties and all the ice cream with which they came in contact; pray put them all on a large plate, and then I will eat them, which will save my having to boil myself an egg later. Now – if I just remove the raven from the knife rack – I do not believe that any more need be said about this matter.'

Aunt Effie looked as if she violently disagreed, but since Lord Donisthorpe was the owner of the zoo she was obliged to give way. Mortimer was much too busy to trouble his head about the furious glances Aunt Effie was giving him; released from the knife rack, he sat on the red plastic table between Arabel and Lord Donisthorpe, holding his dandelion ice-cream cone in his claw and studying it admiringly. Then he ate it very fast in one bite and two swallows – crunch, hoosh, swallop – and then he looked round to see what everybody else was doing. Arabel had mostly finished her quince ice cream – which was delicious – but Lord Donisthorpe still had quite a number of cream-cheese patties to go, so Mortimer helped him with four of them.

Meanwhile, at a table by the window, two men, one of them wearing a hat and one not, had been watching this scene, and were now staring thoughtfully at Mortimer.

The hatless man took his teacup and went back to the counter to have it refilled. 'That seems to be a very badly behaved bird,' he said to Aunt Effie, as she handed him his cup and he gave her the money.

'You can say that again,' snapped Aunt Effie. 'He has to stay in my house while my brother-in-law has his veryclose veins operated on, but I certainly intend to see he does as little damage as possible while he's here. The havoc that Monster has wreaked at my brother-in-law's you'd never credit – eaten whole gas stoves and kitchen sinks, he has – worse than a tribe of Tartar Sorcerers, he is! Into the meat safe he goes the minute he gets back to my house, I can tell you.'

'A very sensible plan, madam,' the hatless man agreed. 'And if I were you, I should put that meat safe out of doors. A bird like that can harbour all sorts of infection – it would be downright dangerous to have it in the house.'

'That's true,' said Aunt Effie. 'We could all come down with Raven Delirium, or get Inter-city-cosis from him. I'll put the meat safe out on the front lawn. And if it rains, so much the better; I don't suppose that black Fiend ever had a wash in his life.'

The hatless man went back to the window table with his tea. While he was waiting for it to cool, he said to his friend in a low voice, 'We can pin the blame on the bird. All we have to do is to open the meat safe. Everybody will think that *he* let out the animals.'

Presently the two men left the cafeteria and strolled away, glancing carelessly at the giraffe house, the zebra bower and the ostrich haven as they passed. Then they left the zoo.

Arabel thanked Lord Donisthorpe for her and Mortimer's treats. Lord Donisthorpe patted her head and gave her a tenpenny piece. 'That will buy your raven another doughnut,' he said. 'But I should wait till tomorrow.'

'Oh yes, he's full up now,' said Arabel.

Mortimer, absolutely stuffed with ice cream and cheese patty, made no difficulty about going home to bed.

'I'll be back at the house in twenty minutes,' called Aunt Effie from the counter, where she was washing up the used knives and forks. 'Don't you let that bird touch *anything* in the house. Tell your Uncle Urk I said so.'

Going towards home, Arabel and Mortimer caught up with Uncle Urk, whose jobs were finished and who was intending to watch television.

'Uncle Urk,' said Arabel, 'I think those two men who were in the cafeteria are animal thieves. They were in the same railway carriage with me and Mortimer, and they were talking about zebras and giraffes and ostriches.'

'*Course* they were talking about zebras and giraffes and ostriches, Arabel, dearie,' said Uncle Urk kindly. 'Cos they was a-coming to the zoo,

see? Natural, people talks about zebras and camels and giraffes when they're a-going to *see* ostriches and giraffes and camels.'

'I think they were thieves,' said Arabel. 'Don't you think so, Mortimer?'

'Kaaark,' said Mortimer.

'Can't take what that bird says as evidence,' said Uncle Urk. ''Sides, little gals gets to fancying things, *I* know. Little gals is very fanciful creatures. That's what you bin a-doing, Arabel, dearie – you got to fancying things about animal thieves. We won't mention it to your Aunt Effie, eh, case she gets nervous? Terrible nervous your Aunt Effie can get, once she begins.'

'But, Uncle Urk,' said Arabel.

'Now, Arabel, dearie, don't you trouble your head about such things – *or* mine,' said Uncle Urk, who was dying to watch Rumbury Wanderers play Liverpool United, and he hurried into the house.

Arabel saw that Chris, whose evening jobs were finished, had taken his guitar into Uncle Urk's garden. Arabel and Mortimer loved listening to Chris play, so they went and sat beside him and he sang:

> *'Arabel's raven is quick on the draw,*
> *Better steer clear of his beak and his claw,*
> *When there is trouble, you know in your bones,*
> *Right in the middle is Mortimer Jones!'*

Mortimer drew himself up and looked immensely proud that a song had been written about him. Arabel sucked her finger and leaned against an apple tree.

Inside the house, Uncle Urk suddenly thought: 'What if Arabel was right about those men being giraffe thieves? Ben says she's mostly a sensible little thing. I'd look silly if she'd a-warned me, and I didn't do anything, and they really was thieves.'

So, after thinking about it for a while, he rang up Sam Heyward, the nightwatchman, on the zoo internal telephone. 'Sam,' he said, 'I got a kind of a feeling there might be a bit o' trouble tonight, so why don't you let old Noah loose? It's months since he had a night out. You never know, if there's any miscreants abouts, he might put a spoke in their wheel.'

'OK, Urk, if you say so,' said Sam. 'Anyways, old Noah might catch a few rabbits; there's a sight too many rabbits in the park just now, eating up all the wildebeest food.'

Sam left his nightwatchman's hut to let out Noah the boa, who was very pleased to have the freedom of the park again, and slithered quietly away through the grass. When Sam returned to his hut, he didn't notice that a small tube had been slipped under the door, in the crack at the hinge end. As soon as he shut the door a sweet-smelling gas began to dribble in through the tube. By slow degrees Sam became drowsier and drowsier, until, after about half an hour, he toppled right off his stool and lay on the matting fast asleep, dreaming that he had put ten pounds on a horse in the Derby called Horseradish, and that it had been on the point of winning when Noah the boa, who could travel at a terrific speed when he chose to, suddenly shot under the tape just ahead of Horseradish, and won the race.

Meanwhile, in Uncle Urk's garden, Chris sang,

'Arabel's raven is perfectly hollow,
What he can't chew up he'll manage to swallow –
Furniture – fire escapes – fencing – and phones –
All are digested by Mortimer Jones.'

Mortimer looked even prouder.
Chris sang,

'When the ice cream disappears from the cones,
When you are deafened by shrieks or by moans,
When the fur's flying, or the air's full of stones,
You can be certain –'

Just at this moment Aunt Effie came home. As soon as she was through the gate, she said: 'Chris! Fetch out that meat safe!'

Looking rather startled, Chris laid down his guitar and did as he was told. He placed the meat safe under the apple tree.

Instantly, Aunt Effie grabbed Mortimer, thrust him into the safe (which he completely filled), shut the door, and slammed home the catch.

A fearful cry came from inside.

'There!' said Aunt Effie. 'Now, you go up to bed, Arabel Jones, and I don't want to hear a *single sound* out of you, or out of that bird, till morning – do you hear me?'

Since Mortimer, inside the meat safe, was making a noise like a troop of roller skaters crossing a tin bridge, and shouting 'Nevermore!'

at the top of his lungs, it was quite hard for Arabel to hear what Aunt Effie said, but she could easily understand what her aunt meant.

Arabel went quietly and sadly up to bed, but she had not the least intention of leaving Mortimer to pass the night inside the meat safe. 'He hasn't done anything bad in Aunt Effie's house,' Arabel thought. 'So why should he be punished by being shut inside the meat safe? It isn't fair. Besides, Mortimer can't stand being shut up.'

Indeed, the noise from the meat safe could be heard for two hundred yards around Uncle Urk's house. But Aunt Effie went indoors and turned up the volume of the television very loud, in order to drown Mortimer's yells and bangs.

'When he learns who's master he'll soon settle down,' she said grimly.

Arabel always did exactly as she was told. Aunt Effie had said, 'I don't want to hear a single sound out of you,' so, as soon as it was dark, and Aunt Effie and Uncle Urk had gone to bed, Arabel put on her dressing gown and slippers and went very softly down the stairs and out through the front door, which she had to unlock. She did not make a single sound.

Mortimer had quieted down, just a little, inside the meat safe, but he was very far from asleep. He was making a miserable mumbling groaning to himself, and kicking and scratching with his claws. Arabel softly undid the catch.

'Hush, Mortimer!' she whispered. 'We don't want to wake them.'

They could hear Uncle Urk's snores coming out through the bedroom window. The sound was like somebody grinding a bunch of rusty wires along a section of corrugated iron, ending with a tremendous rattle.

Mortimer was so glad to see Arabel that he went quite silent. She lifted him out of the meat safe and held him tight, flattening his feathers, which were all endways and ruffled. Then she carried him back up the stairs to the bedroom.

Mortimer did not usually like sleeping on a bed; he preferred a bread bin or a coal scuttle or the airing cupboard; but he had been so horrified

by the meat safe that he was happy to share Arabel's eiderdown, though he did peck a hole in it so that most of the feathers came out. Either because of all the feathers flying around, or because of the excitements of the day, neither Arabel nor Mortimer slept very well.

Mortimer was dreaming about giraffes. Arabel was dreaming about Noah the boa.

After an hour or so, Mortimer suddenly shot bolt upright in bed.

'What is it, Mortimer?' whispered Arabel. She knew that Mortimer's ears were very keen, like those of an owl; he could hear a potato crisp fall on to a carpeted floor half a mile away.

Mortimer turned his head, intently listening. Now even Arabel thought she could hear something, past Uncle Urk's snores – a soft series of muffled thumps.

'Oh, my goodness, Mortimer! Do you think those men are stealing Lord Donisthorpe's giraffes?'

Mortimer did think so. His boot-button black eyes gleamed with pleasure at the thought. Arabel could see this because the moon was shining brightly through the window.

'I had better wake up Uncle Urk,' said Arabel. 'Though Aunt Effie will be cross, because she said she didn't want to hear me.'

She went and tapped on Uncle Urk's door and said in a soft, polite voice, so as not to disturb Aunt Effie: 'Uncle Urk. Would you come out, please? We believe that thieves are stealing your giraffes.'

But the noise made by Uncle Urk as he snored was so tremendous that neither he nor Aunt Effie (who was snoring a bit on her own account) could hear Arabel's polite tones.

'Oh dear, Mortimer,' said Arabel, then. 'I wonder what we had better do.'

Mortimer plainly thought that they ought to let well alone. His expression suggested that if every giraffe in the zoo were hijacked he, personally, would not raise any objection.

'Perhaps we could wake up Lord Donisthorpe,' Arabel said, and she went downstairs and into the garden, with Mortimer sitting on her shoulder.

But when they were close to it, Lord Donisthorpe's castle looked very difficult to enter. There was a moat, and a drawbridge, which was raised, and a massive wooden door, which was shut.

Then Arabel remembered that Chris slept in a wooden hut near the ostrich enclosure.

'We'll wake Chris,' she told Mortimer. 'He'll know what to do.'

Mortimer was greatly enjoying the trip through the moonlit zoo. He did not mind where they went, or what they did, so long as they did not go back to bed too soon.

Arabel walked quietly over the grass in her bedroom slippers. 'Chris sleeps in the hut with red geraniums in the window boxes,' she said. 'He showed it to me while the doughnuts were cooking.'

'Kaaark,' said Mortimer, thinking about doughnuts.

Arabel walked up to the hut with the red geraniums and banged on the door.

'Chris!' she called softly. 'It's me – Arabel! Will you open the door, please?'

It took a long time to wake Chris. Nobody had pumped any gas under his door; he was just naturally a very heavy sleeper. But at last he woke and came stumbling and yawning to open the door. He was very surprised to see Arabel.

'Arabel! And Mortimer! Whatever are you doing up at this time of night? Your Aunt Effie would blow her top!'

'Shhhh!' said Arabel. 'Chris, Mortimer and I think there are thieves in the zoo. Can't you hear a kind of thumping and bumping, coming from the zebra house?'

Chris listened and thought he could. 'I'd best set off the alarm,' he said. 'Lord Donisthorpe always tells us, better ten false alarms than lose one animal.'

He pressed the alarm button, which ought to have let off tremendously loud sirens at different points all over the park. But nothing happened.

'That's funny,' Chris said, scratching his head and yawning some more. Then his eyes and his mouth opened wide, and he said: 'Blimey! It *must* be thieves. They must have cut the wire. I'd best go on my bike and rouse Lord Donisthorpe – I know a back way into the castle, and then he can phone the police. *You*'d better stop here, Arabel, until I get back; you shouldn't be running about the zoo in your slippers if there's thieves around.'

Chris started off on his bike towards Lord Donisthorpe's castle. Arabel would have stayed in his hut, as he asked her, but Mortimer had other ideas. He hoisted himself off Arabel's shoulder and began flapping heavily along the ground in the direction of the giraffe house.

'Mortimer!' called Arabel. 'Come back!'

But Mortimer took no notice, and so Arabel started in pursuit of him.

To Arabel's horror, as she went after Mortimer, she saw a truck parked outside the zebra house. Men with black bowler hats crammed so far down over their heads that their faces were invisible, stood by the truck packing in limp zebras, which seemed to be fast asleep.

'Oh, how awful!' said Arabel. 'Mortimer, stop! The thieves are stealing the zebras!'

But Mortimer was not interested in zebra thieves. He had only one idea in his head and that was to get to the doughnut machine near the giraffe house. The thieves did not notice Arabel and Mortimer pass by, and Arabel caught up with Mortimer just as he perched on the machine.

'Kaaark!' he said, giving the machine a hopeful kick.

'If I get you a doughnut, Mortimer, will you come back with me quietly to Chris's hut?' said Arabel. She had the tenpenny piece that Lord Donisthorpe had given her in her dressing-gown pocket.

Mortimer made no answer, but jumped up and down on top of the machine.

So Arabel put her coin in the slot, and Mortimer, almost standing on his head with interest and enthusiasm, watched the doughnut slide down into the oil to cook; then he watched the hook hoist it out and the puffer blow white crystals all over it; then he watched it tumble out into the paper cup; then he grabbed it, jumped down off the machine, and disappeared in the direction of the giraffe house.

'Mortimer, come back!' called Arabel. 'You promised –!'

But that was all she said, for next minute she found herself wrapped up as tightly as if twenty yards of oil pipeline had been wound round her, and she found herself staring, stiff with fright, straight into the thoughtful face of Noah the boa.

Meanwhile the thieves, working at top speed, had packed all the drugged zebras into their truck, with layers of foam rubber in between. Then they went on to the ostriches. It was easy to drug the ostriches; all they needed to do was sprinkle chloroform on the sand where the ostriches hid their heads, and then make an alarming noise; in five minutes all the ostriches were flat out.

'D'you reckon we've time to take in a few camels as well as the giraffes?' asked Fred the truck driver, when the ostriches were packed in. 'Camels are fetching very fancy prices just now, up Blackpool way.'

But the short fat man was looking towards Lord Donisthorpe's castle, where a light had come on in one of the windows, high up.

'That looks like trouble,' he said. 'Maybe the old geezer heard something. We better not fool around; go straight for the giraffes, get them packed in, and get away.'

At this moment, Lord Donisthorpe was speaking on the phone to the local police. 'Yes, Inspector; as I just told you, we have reason to believe that there are thieves on my estate, engaged in stealing animals – *who* told me so? I understand that a raven, of unusually acute hearing, informed a young person named Arabel Jones, who informed a youthful attendant at the zoo – who informed *me* –'

At this moment also, Noah the boa, who had decided, after careful inspection of Arabel, that she looked as if she might be good to eat, probably not *quite* as good as a doughnut, but still much better than a rabbit, had thrown an extra loop of himself round both Arabel and the doughnut machine, to which he was hitched, and had begun

to squeeze, at the same time opening his mouth wider and wider.

But his squeezing had an unexpected effect. It started the doughnut machine working, just as if somebody had put in a coin.

Arabel, doing her best to keep quite calm, said politely, 'Excuse me: but if you wouldn't mind undoing the coil that is holding my hands, *here*, I would be able to press the lever and then I could get you a doughnut, if you'd like?'

Noah was not very bright, but he did understand the word *doughnut*, and Arabel's wriggling of her hands indicated what she meant. He loosened one of his coils; Arabel pressed the lever twice; and the machine, ever so quickly, sugared a doughnut and tossed it out into a paper cup. Noah swallowed it in a flash, and, as the machine was still working, Arabel pressed the lever again.

Meanwhile the thieves had quietly moved their truck on to the giraffe house, parked, and gone inside.

'*Blimey*,' said Fred, 'what, in the name of all that's 'orrible, 'as been going on 'ere?'

For when they shone their torches around, a scene of perfectly hopeless confusion was revealed: all that could be seen was legs of giraffes at the bottom of the spiral stair, while their necks, like some dreadfully tangled piece of knitting, were all twined up inside the spiral.

'Strewth!' said the short fat man. 'How are we *ever* going to get them out of there?'

Meanwhile Lord Donisthorpe and Chris, both riding bicycles, were dashing through the zoo, hunting for the malefactors. Chris was dreadfully worried about Arabel, because he had found his hut empty; he kept calling, as he rode along, 'Arabel? Mortimer? Where are you?'

At this moment the thieves, feverishly trying to untangle the necks of the giraffes and drag them out of the spiral stair, heard the unmistakable gulping howl of a police-car siren, coming fast.

'Here, we better scarper,' said the fat man.

'They got cops in helicopters?' said Fred. 'The sound o' that siren seems to be coming from dead overhead.'

'It's the acoustics of this building, thickhead.'

'Never mind where the perishing sound's *coming* from,' said the pale man. 'We better hop it. At least we've got the ostriches and the zebras.'

They ran for their truck. But Chris, who reached it just before them, had taken the key out of the ignition. The thieves were obliged to abandon their van and escape on foot. And as they pounded towards the distant gate, something like a main drain travelling at thirty miles an hour caught up with them, flung a half-hitch round each of them, and brought them to the ground.

It was Noah who, having, for once in his life, eaten as many doughnuts as he wanted, was now prepared to do his job of burglar-catching.

Chris went in search of Arabel and found her, rather pale and faint, sitting by the doughnut machine. Mortimer, looking very pleased with himself indeed, was perched on her shoulder, still giving his celebrated imitation of a police-car siren. When the real police turned up, half an hour later, all they had to do was take the thieves off to jail. Then, greatly to Arabel's relief, Lord

Donisthorpe took Noah back to his cage, wheeling him in a barrow.

Chris and Lord Donisthorpe had already unpacked the ostriches and zebras and laid them out in the fresh air to sleep off the effects of the drug they had been given.

But it took ever so much longer to untangle the giraffes from the spiral stair. In fact they were obliged to dismantle the top part of the stair altogether.

'I can't think how they ever *got* their necks in like this,' said Lord Donisthorpe, panting. 'Let alone *why*.'

Chris thought he could guess. He had found traces of doughnut on each step all the way up.

'Perhaps it's not such a good plan to have a spiral stair in the giraffe house,' murmured Lord Donisthorpe, as the last captive – Wendy – was carefully pulled out, set upright on her spindly legs, and given a pail of giraffe food to revive her.

'Well, I certainly am greatly obliged to you three,' added Lord Donisthorpe to Arabel and Chris, who had helped to extract Wendy, and to Mortimer, who had been sitting on the stair rail and enjoying the spectacle. 'But for you, my zoo

would have suffered severe losses tonight, and I hope I can do something for you in return.'

Chris said politely that he didn't think he wanted anything. He just liked working in the zoo.

Mortimer didn't even bother to reply. He was remembering how enjoyable it had been to entice Wendy, Elsie and Derek further and further up the spiral stair by holding the doughnut just in front of their noses.

But Arabel said, 'Oh, please, Lord Donisthorpe. Could you please ask Aunt Effie *not* to shut Mortimer up in the meat safe? He does hate it so.'

'Perhaps it would be best,' said Lord Donisthorpe thoughtfully, 'if Mortimer came to stay with me in my castle while you remain at Foxwell. I believe ravens are often to be found in castles. And there is really very little harm he can do there. If any.'

'Oh, *yes*,' said Arabel. 'He'd *love* to live in a castle, wouldn't you, Mortimer?'

'Kaaark,' said Mortimer.

And so that is what happened.

Aunt Effie and Uncle Urk were quite astonished when they woke up next morning and learned all that had been going on during the night. But Aunt Effie was not able to scold Arabel or Mortimer, as Lord Donisthorpe said they had been the means of saving all his ostriches and zebras, not to mention the giraffes.

Arabel soon became very fond of Wendy, Derek and Elsie; though she had continual trouble preventing Mortimer from teasing them.

But she never did get to like Noah the boa.

Mortimer and the
Sword Excalibur

IT WAS A fine spring morning in Rainwater Crescent, Rumbury Town, north London. Arabel Jones, and Mortimer, Arabel's raven, were sitting on Arabel's bedroom windowsill, which was a very wide and comfortable one, with plenty of room for them both, and a cushion as well. They were both looking out of the window, watching the work that was going on across the road in Rainwater Crescent Garden.

This garden, which was quite large, went most of the way along the inside of Rainwater Crescent, which curved round like a banana. So the garden was curved on one side and straight on the other, like a section from an enormous orange. In it

there were ten trees, quite a wide lawn, some flower beds, six benches, two statues, a sandpit for children and a flat paved bit in the middle, where a band sometimes played.

Arabel liked spending the afternoon in Rainwater Garden, but she was not allowed to go there on her own, because of crossing the street. However sometimes Mrs Jones took her across and left her, if Mr Walpole, the Rumbury Town municipal gardener, was there to keep an eye on her.

Today a whole lot of interesting things were happening in the garden, directly across the road from the Jones's house.

Before breakfast a huge excavator with a long metal neck and a pair of grabbing jaws like a crocodile had come trundling along the road. And it had started in at once, very fast, digging a deep hole. This was to be the entrance to an underground car park, which was going to be right underneath Rainwater Crescent Garden. The excavator had dug its deep hole at the end of the garden where the children's sandpit used to be. Arabel was sorry about that; so was Mortimer. They had been fond of playing in the sandpit. Arabel liked building castles; Mortimer liked jumping on them and flattening them out. Also he liked burrowing deep in the sand, working it in thoroughly among his feathers, and then waiting till he was home to shake himself out. But now there was a hole as deep as a house where the sandpit had been, and a lot of men standing round the edge of it, talking to each other and waving their arms in a very excited manner, while the excavator stood idly beside them, doing nothing, and hanging its head like a horse that wants its nosebag.

While the excavator had been at work digging, a large crowd of people had collected to watch it. Now it had stopped, they had all wandered off and were doing different things in the Crescent

Garden. Some were flying kites. The kites were all kinds – like boats, like birds, like fish, and some that were just long silvery streamers which very easily got caught in trees and hung there flapping. Mr Walpole the gardener hated that sort, because they looked untidy in the trees, and the owners were always climbing up to rescue them, and breaking branches. Other people were skipping with skipping ropes. Others were skating on skateboards, along the paved bit in the middle of the lawn where the band sometimes played. This was just right for skateboards, as it sloped up slightly at each end, which gave the skaters a good start, and they were doing beautiful things, turning and gliding and whizzing and jumping up into the air, and weaving past each other very cleverly.

Arabel specially loved watching the skaters.

'Oh, please, Ma,' she said to her mother who came into the bedroom presently, and started rummaging crossly about in Arabel's clothes cupboard, 'Oh, please, Ma, couldn't Mortimer and I have a skateboard? I *would* like one, ever so much, and so would Mortimer, wouldn't you, Mortimer?'

But Mortimer was looking out of the window very intently, and did not reply.

'A *skateboard*?' said Mrs Jones, who seemed put out about something. 'In the name of goodness, what will you think of next; I should think *not*, indeed! Nasty dangerous things, break your leg as soon as look at them, ought to be banned by Act of Parking-Lot, they should, banging into people's shins and shopping baskets in the High Street. Oh my dear cats alive, *now* what am I going to do? Granny Jones has just phoned to say she'll be coming tomorrow morning, and your blue velveteen pinafore at the cleaner's because of that time Mortimer got excited with the éclairs at Penny Conway's birthday party; and I haven't yet made you a dress out of that piece of pink georgette that Granny Jones brought for you last time she came; I'll just have to run it up into a frock for you now; why ever in the world can't Granny Jones give us a bit more *notice* before she comes on a visit, I'd like to ask? There's the best sheets at the laundry, too, oh dear, I don't know I'm sure –'

And Mrs Jones bustled off down the stairs again.

Arabel wrapped her arms round her knees. She liked Granny Jones, but the pink georgette sounded very chilly; Arabel hated having new clothes tried on, because of the draughts, and her mother's cold hands, and the pins that sometimes got stuck in her; besides, she would much rather have gone on wearing her jeans and sweater.

Mortimer the raven had taken no notice of this conversation. He was sitting as quiet as a mushroom, watching Mr Walpole the gardener, who had gone to the shed where he kept his tools, and wheeled out an enormous grass-cutting machine called a LawnSabre.

Just now, this LawnSabre was Mortimer's favourite thing in the whole world, and he spent a lot of every day hoping that he would see Mr Walpole using it. What Mortimer wanted even more was to be allowed to drive the LawnSabre himself. It was not at all likely that he *would* be allowed; firstly, the LawnSabre was very dangerous, because it had two terribly sharp blades that whirled round and round underneath. It was covered all over with warning notices in large print: DO NOT USE THIS MACHINE UNLESS WEARING DOUBLE-THICK LEATHER BOOTS WITH METAL TOECAPS. NEVER ALLOW THIS MACHINE NEAR CHILDREN. DO NOT RUN THIS MACHINE BACKWARDS OR SIDEWAYS OR UPHILL OR DOWNHILL. NEVER TRY TO LIFT THIS MACHINE UNTIL THE BLADES HAVE COMPLETELY

STOPPED TURNING. Secondly, Mr Walpole was very particular indeed about his machine, and never let anybody else touch it, even humans, let alone ravens.

Now Mr Walpole was starting it up. First he turned a couple of switches. Then, very energetically, he pulled out a long string half a dozen times. At about the eighth or ninth pull, the machine suddenly let out a loud chattering roar. Mortimer watched all this very closely; his head was stuck forward, and his black boot-button eyes were bright with interest. Next, Mr Walpole wheeled the LawnSabre on to the grass, keeping his booted feet well out of its way. He pulled a lever, and pushed the machine off across the lawn, leaving a long stripe of neat short grass behind, like a staircarpet, as the blades underneath whirled round, shooting out a shower of cut grass blades.

'Kaaark,' said Mortimer gently to himself, and he began to jump up and down.

'It's no use, Mortimer,' said Arabel, who guessed what he meant. 'I'm afraid Mr Walpole would never let you push his mower.'

'Nevermore,' said Mortimer.

'Why don't you watch Sandy Smith?' said Arabel. 'He's doing a lot of lovely things.'

Mortimer sank his head into his neck feathers in a very dejected manner. He was not interested in Sandy Smith; and Mr Walpole was now far away, over on the opposite side of the paved central area where the skaters were skating.

Arabel, however, paid careful attention to the things that Sandy Smith was doing. He was a boy who lived in Rainwater Crescent, next door but three to the Joneses, and he was training to go into a circus. He had come out into the Crescent Garden to practise his act, and he was doing tricks with three balls.

He was throwing them up into the air, one after another, and catching them with a hand under his

knee, or behind his back, or in his mouth, or under his chin, or bouncing them off his knee, his elbow, his nose, the top of his head, or the sole of his foot; meanwhile he played a tune on a nose organ which was clipped to his nose.

Arabel thought Sandy very clever indeed, though she could not hear the tune because of the noise made by Mr Walpole's mower. But Mortimer was still watching Mr Walpole, who had now worked his way round to this side of the garden again.

'Arabel, dearie,' called her mother. 'Come down here a minute, I want to measure you before I cut out your dress. You've grown at least an inch since I made your blue.'

'*You'd* better come too, Mortimer,' said Arabel.

'Nevermore,' grumbled Mortimer, who would sooner have stayed on the windowsill watching Mr Walpole cutting the grass. But Arabel picked him up and tucked him firmly under her arm. Left to himself, Mortimer had been known to chew all the putty out from the window frame, so that the glass fell out into the front garden.

Arabel carried Mortimer down the stairs into the dining room. There, Mrs Jones had pulled out her pedal sewing machine from where it stood by the wall, and taken off the lid; and on the dining table she had laid out a long strip of pale flimsy pink material. It looked very thin and chilly to Arabel.

'Take your cardigan off, dearie,' said Mrs Jones. 'I want to measure round your middle.'

Arabel put Mortimer on the windowsill. But this window looked out into the Joneses' back garden, where nothing interesting was happening. Mortimer flopped across on to a chair, and began studying Mrs Jones's sewing machine.

A sewing machine was not a LawnSabre; but it was better than nothing. At least it was *there*, right in the room.

'Kaaark,' said Mortimer thoughtfully to himself.

Arabel slowly took off her nice thick, warm cardigan.

Mortimer inspected the sewing machine. It had a bobbin of pink thread on top, a big wheel at the right-hand end, a lot of silvery twiddles at the other end, and a needle that went up and down between the metal toes of a two-pronged foot.

'Ma –' said Arabel, when she had been measured, and put on her cardigan again – the cardigan felt cold now – 'Ma, couldn't you take Mortimer and me across the road into the Crescent Garden? Sandy's there, juggling, and Mr Walpole too, he'd keep an eye on us –'

'No time just now,' said Mrs Jones, through one corner of her mouth – the rest of her mouth was pressed tight on a row of pins – 'besides, I'll be wanting to measure again in a minute. Why can't you play in the back garden, nicely, with your spade and fork?'

'Because we want to watch Sandy and Mr Walpole,' said Arabel.

'Kaark,' said Mortimer. He wanted to watch the LawnSabre.

'Well, if you want to watch you'd better go back upstairs,' said Mrs Jones. 'I'll need you again as soon as I've sewn up the skirt.'

She laid a piece of paper pattern over the pink stuff on the table, pinned it on with some of the pins from her mouth, and started quickly snipping round the edge. The scissors made a gritty scrunching noise along the table; every now and then Mrs Jones stopped to make a snick in the edge of the pink stuff. Then, when she had two large fan-shaped pieces cut out, she unpinned the paper pattern from them, pinned them to each other, and slid them under the metal foot of the sewing machine.

'What are those pieces?' asked Arabel.

'That's the back and front of the skirt,' said Mrs Jones, sitting down at the sewing machine and starting to work the pedal with her foot.

Mortimer could not see this from where he sat. But he saw the bobbin of pink thread on top of the machine suddenly start to spin round. The big wheel turned, and the needle flashed up and down. The pieces of pink skirt suddenly shot backwards on to the floor.

'Kaaark,' said Mortimer, much interested.

'Drat!' said Mrs Jones. 'Left the machine in reverse. That's what comes of answering questions. Do run along, Arabel, duck; and take Mortimer with you. It makes me nervous when he's in the room; I'm always expecting him to do something horrible.'

Arabel picked up Mortimer (who had indeed begun to sidle towards Mrs Jones's biscuit tin full of red and brown and pink and blue and green and white and yellow cotton reels, after studying them in a very thoughtful manner). She carried him upstairs, and put him back on her bedroom windowsill.

Across the road, in Rainwater Crescent Garden, the big excavator was still idly hanging its head, while the group of men still stood on the edge of the huge crater it had dug, arguing and waving their hands about. Sometimes one or another of them would climb down a ladder and vanish into the hole.

'Perhaps they've found a dinosaur down there,' said Arabel. 'I do wish we could see to the bottom of the hole.'

But the hole was too deep for that. From where they sat, they could see only a bit of the side.

Mr Walpole, pushing the LawnSabre, had now cut a wide circle of grass all round the paved middle section. And Sandy the juggler had put away his three balls. Instead he had lit three flaming torches, which he was tossing into the air and catching, just as easily as if they were not shooting out plumes of red and yellow fire.

'*Coo*, Mortimer,' said Arabel. 'Look at that!'

'Kaaark,' said Mortimer. But he was really much more interested in following the course of Mr Walpole and the LawnSabre. He was remembering a plane that he had once seen take off at London Airport, when the family went to say goodbye to Aunt Flossie from Toronto; and he was hoping that Mr Walpole and the LawnSabre would presently take right off into the air.

Now Sandy the juggler stuck his three torches into a patch of loose earth, where they continued to burn. He pulled a long piece of rope out of his kit bag, which lay beside him on the ground. Looking round, he saw a plane tree that grew on a piece of lawn already mowed by Mr Walpole. Sandy ran to this tree, climbed up it like a squirrel, tied one end of his rope quite high up its trunk, and jumped down again. Then, going to a second tree that grew about twenty feet from the first, he climbed up and tied the other end of the rope to *that* tree.

'He's put up a clothes line,' said Arabel, poking Mortimer. 'That's funny! Do you think he's going to hang up some washing, Mortimer?'

'Kaaark,' said Mortimer, not paying much attention. He had his eye on Mr Walpole and the LawnSabre.

But now Sandy climbed back up the first tree, carrying two of his three torches in his teeth. And then he began to walk very slowly along the rope, holding on to it with his toes, and balancing himself with his arms spread out. In each hand was a flaming torch.

'*Look*, Mortimer,' said Arabel. 'He's walking on the *rope*!'

Mortimer *was* quite amazed at that. He looked at Sandy balancing on the rope, and muttered 'Nevermore,' to himself.

'Bet *you* couldn't do that, Mortimer,' said Arabel.

However at this moment Sandy dropped one of his torches, and Mr Walpole shouted, ''Ere, you! Don't you singe my turf, young feller, or I'll singe *you*, good and proper!'

So Sandy jumped down again, put away his torches, and went up with a long rod instead. Holding each end of this with his hands stretched out wide apart, he began slowly walking along the rope once more.

'Arabel, dearie, will you come downstairs?' called Mrs Jones. 'I've sewn up the skirt, and I want to try it on you for length.'

'Oh, please, Ma,' said Arabel, 'I want to watch Sandy. He's doing ever such interesting things. He's walking along the rope. Must I come just now?'

'Yes, you must!' called Mrs Jones sharply. 'I've a lot to do and I haven't got all day. Come along down at once and bring that feathered wretch

with you, else he'll get up to mischief if he's left
alone.'

Arabel picked up Mortimer and went slowly
downstairs again.

Mrs Jones wrapped the pink skirt round Arabel,
over her jeans, and then led her out into the front
hall, where there was a long mirror.

'Stand still and don't wriggle while I pin it up,'
she said, with her mouth full of pins. 'Stand up
straight, Arabel, can't you? I want to pin the hem,
and I can't if you keep leaning over sideways.'

Arabel was trying to see what Mortimer was
doing; she had left him on the dining-room table.

'Mortimer?' she called.

But while Mrs Jones was pinning up the skirt hem, Mortimer was carefully studying all the pieces of pink material on the table. He swallowed a good many of them. Then, deciding that they did not taste interesting, he flopped quickly across from the table to Mrs Jones's sewing machine. Remembering the way that Mr Walpole started the LawnSabre, by pulling a string, he tried to start the sewing machine by giving a tremendous tug to the pink thread that dangled down through the eye of the needle.

Nothing happened, except that he undid a whole lot of thread, and the bobbin whirled round and round.

Soon there was a thick tangle of thread, like a swan's nest, all round the sewing machine, as Mortimer tugged and tugged. But still the machine would not start.

'Nevermore,' muttered Mortimer irritably.

At last, after he had given a particularly vigorous tug, the needle broke off, and the bottom half came sliding down the thread on its eye. So then Mortimer swallowed the needle.

Giving up on the thread, he then tried pushing round the big wheel with his claw. Then he tried unscrewing a knob on top of the machine. Nothing happened, so he swallowed the knob.

Then he pushed up a metal flap, under where the needle had been, and stuck his beak into the hole under the flap. The beak would not go in very far, so he poked in his claw, which came out with a shiny metal spindle on it; so Mortimer swallowed this too. But as he *still* had not managed to start the sewing machine, he finally gave it up in disgust, flopped down on to the floor, and walked off into the front hall, just as Mrs Jones finished pinning the hem of Arabel's skirt.

'*That*'s done, then,' said Mrs Jones. 'I'll hem it up this afternoon. Now we'd better have a bite to eat, or that bird will get up to mischief; he always does when he's hungry. Shut the dining-room door, Arabel, so he can't get in; you can hang your skirt over the ironing board in the kitchen.'

Arabel, Mortimer and Mrs Jones had their lunch in the kitchen. Mrs Jones and Arabel had tomato soup and battered fish fingers. Mortimer did not care for soup; he just had the fish fingers, and he battered his even more, by throwing them into the air, chopping them in half with his beak as they came down, and then jumping on them to make them really squashy.

After that they had bananas.

Mortimer unpeeled his banana by pecking the peel at the stalk end, and then, firmly holding on to the stalk, he whirled the banana round and round his head, like a sling thrower.

'*Mortimer!* You must go outside if you want to do that!' said Mrs Jones, but she said it just too late. Mortimer's banana shot out of its skin and flew through the air; it became stuck among the bristles of the stiff broom, which was leaning upside down against the kitchen wall. Mrs Jones was very annoyed about this, but not nearly so annoyed as Mortimer, who had a very difficult time picking bits of banana out from among the broom bristles.

Mrs Jones refused to give him another.

'When three bananas cost forty pence?' she said. 'Are you joking? He must just make do with what he can get out.'

When they had washed up the lunch dishes and Mrs Jones went back into the dining room and discovered what Mortimer had been doing, there was a fearful scene.

'Just wait till I get my hands on that blessed bird!' shrieked Mrs Jones. 'I'll put him in the dustbin and shut the lid on him! I'll scour him with a Scrubbo pad! I'll spray him with oven spray!'

'Kaaark,' said Mortimer, who was sitting on the dining-room mantelpiece.

'I'll kaaark you, my boy. I'll make you kaaark on the other side of your face!'

However Mrs Jones was really in too much of a hurry to finish making Arabel's dress and tidy the house before the arrival of Granny Jones to carry out any of her threats.

She cut off the tangle of pink thread and threw it all away; she put a new needle and spindle on to the machine, replaced the knob on top from her box of spare parts, set the needle to hem, and put Arabel's skirt under the foot. Then she started to sew.

Mrs Jones's sewing machine was not new; and Mortimer's treatment had upset it; it began doing terrible things. It stuck fast with a loud grinding noise, it puckered up the pink material, it refused to sew at all, or poured out great handfuls of thread, and then sewed in enormously wide stitches, which hardly held the cloth together.

'*Drat* that Mortimer,' muttered Mrs Jones, furiously putting Arabel's pink waistband under the foot to sew it for the third time, after she had ripped out all the loose stitching. 'I wish he was at the bottom of the sea, that I do!'

Suddenly the machine began sewing all by itself, very fast, before Mrs Jones was ready for it.

'*Now* what's the matter with it?' cried Mrs Jones. 'Has it gone bewitched?'

'Mortimer's on the pedal, Ma,' said Arabel.

Mortimer had at last discovered what made the machine go. He was sitting on the foot-pedal, and making the needle race very fast, in a zig-zag course, along the pink waistband.

'*Get* off there!' said Mrs Jones, and she would have removed Mortimer from the pedal with her foot, if he had not removed himself very speedily, and gone back to the mantelpiece.

'Ma, couldn't Mortimer and I go into Rainwater Garden now?' said Arabel. 'You've done the trying-on, and you needn't come across the road with us, you could just watch to see we go when there's no traffic. And Mr Walpole's there, he'd keep an eye on us. And Sandy's still there doing tricks. And you know you sew ever so much better when Mortimer isn't around.'

'I could sew ever so much better if he wasn't in the *world*,' said Mrs Jones. 'Oh, very well! Put on your anorak, then. Anything to get that black Monster out from under my feet.'

So Arabel ran joyfully to get her anorak and her skipping rope, while Mortimer jumped up and down a great many times, shouting 'Nevermore!' with great enthusiasm and satisfaction.

Then Mrs Jones watched them safe across the road and through the gate into Rainwater Garden.

'Don't you go far from the gate, now!' she called. 'And don't you get near that Bullroarer, Arabel! I don't want you chopped up, or squashed flat, or falling down that big hole it's dug.'

'What about Mortimer?'

'I don't care *what* happens to him,' said Mrs Jones.

Just inside the gate of Rainwater Crescent Garden, Mr Walpole the gardener was standing, talking to a bald man.

'Hullo, Mr Walpole,' said Arabel, running up to him. 'Ma says that Mortimer and me are to be in your charge.'

'That's all right, dearie,' said Mr Walpole absently, listening to what the bald man was saying to him. 'I'll keep an eye on ye. Just don't ye goo near my LawnSabre, that's all . . . Is that so, then, Mr Dunnage, about the hole? That'll put a stop to that-thurr municipal car-park plan, then, I dessay?'

'It certainly will, till we can get someone from the British Museum to come and have a look,' said Mr Dunnage, who was the son of

Lady Dunnage, and taught history at Rumbury Comprehensive, and was also on the Rumbury Historical Preservation Society, and he hurried off to Rumbury Tube Station, to fetch a friend of his from the British Museum.

'Seems they found su'thing val'ble down in that-urr dratted great hole they bin an' dug just whurr my compost heap used to be,' said Mr Walpole. '*I* could'a' told 'em! I allus said 'twould be a mistake to go a-digging in Rainwater Gardens. Stands to reason, if there'd a bin meant to be a car park under thurr, thurr wouldn't a-bin a garden 'ere, dunnit?'

'What did they find down in the hole, Mr Walpole?' said Arabel.

'*I* dunno,' said Mr Walpole. 'Mr Dunnage, 'e said they found su'think that sounded like a sort o' 'sparagus. But *that* can't be right. For one thing, I ain't put *in* no 'sparagus, nor likely to, and second, 'sparagus ain't a root vegetable, let alone you'd never find it down so deep as that.'

And he stumped away, whistling all on one note, to his LawnSabre, which was standing near the paved part in the middle of the garden.

Mortimer instantly started walking after Mr Walpole with such a meaningful expression that

Arabel said quickly: 'Come on, Mortimer, let's see if we can find out what the valuable thing is at the bottom of the deep hole. Maybe it's treasure!'

And she picked up Mortimer and carried him in the other direction.

'Kaaark,' said Mortimer, twisting his head round disappointedly.

But when they reached the edge of the enormous hole, even Mortimer was so interested that, for a time, he almost forgot about the LawnSabre. The hole was so deep that a guard rail had been rigged up round the edge, and a series of ladders led down to the bottom. Standing by the rail and looking over, Arabel and Mortimer could just see down as far as the bottom, where about a dozen people were craning and pushing to look at something in the middle.

'What have they found down there?' Arabel asked a boy with a skateboard, who was standing beside her.

'Somebody said it was a round table,' said the boy.

'A *table*? *That* doesn't sound very valuable,' said Arabel, disappointed. 'I thought they'd found something like a king's crown. Why should a table be valuable? Why should a table be down at the bottom of a hole?'

'*I* dunno,' said the boy. 'Maybe it's a vegy-table! Ha, ha, ha!' And he stepped on to his skateboard, pushed off and glided away down the path. Arabel gazed after him with envy. But Mortimer, staring down into the great crater, was struggling and straining in Arabel's arms. He wanted to go down the ladder and see for himself what was at the bottom.

'*No*, Mortimer,' said Arabel. '*You* can't go down there. How would you get back? You'd have to fly, and you know you don't like that. Come

and see what Sandy's doing. He's got his fiery torches again.'

She carried the unwilling Mortimer back to the circle of watchers round Sandy Smith, who was now swallowing great gulps of fire from his blazing torches, and then spitting them out again.

'Coo, he *is* clever,' said Arabel. 'How would you like to do that, Mortimer?'

'Nevermore,' muttered Mortimer.

He would swallow almost *any*thing, so long as it was hard; but fire always made him nervous, and he edged backwards when Sandy blew out a mouthful of flame.

Then Sandy stuck his fiery torches into the loose earth of a flower bed, and pulled a wheel out of his kit bag. The wheel was a bit bigger than an LP disc, and it had a pedal on each side. Sandy put his feet on the pedals, and suddenly – *whizz* – he began to cycle round and round inside the ring of people who were watching. He made it look very easy, by sticking his hands into his pockets, and playing a tune on his nose organ as he pedalled along. Then he began to go faster and faster, leaning inwards on the bends like a tree blown by the wind. Everybody clapped like mad, and Mortimer jumped up and down. He had wriggled out of Arabel's arms, and was standing on the ground beside her.

Then Sandy noticed Arabel, standing among the watchers.

'Hi, Arabel,' he said, 'like a ride on my shoulders?'

'*Could* I?' said Arabel.

'Why not?' said Sandy. 'Come on!' He stepped off his wheel – which at once fell over on its side – picked up Arabel, and perched her on his shoulders, with a foot dangling forward on each side of his face.

'Hold on tight!' he said.

'*Kaaark!*' shouted Mortimer, who did not want to be left behind.

But Sandy, who had not noticed Mortimer, got back on to his wheel and began riding round and round in a circle again. Arabel felt as if she were flying; the wind rushed past her face, and when he went round a tight curve, Sandy leaned over so far that there was nothing between her and the ground.

'Oh, it's lovely!' cried Arabel. 'Mortimer! Look at me, Mortimer!'

But Mortimer was not looking at Arabel. Very annoyed at being left behind, he had turned his black head right round on its neck, and was looking for Mr Walpole and the LawnSabre. Then he started walking purposefully away from the group of people who were watching Sandy.

'Sandy,' said Arabel, as he whizzed round and round, 'why are they getting someone from the British Museum to look at the thing they found in that hole, if it's only a table?'

Arabel thought Sandy must know all about it, as he had been in the garden since breakfast time, and sure enough he did.

'They found a great big round flat stone thing,' he said, pedalling away. 'It's just about as big as this circle I'm making.'

He did another whirl round, and Arabel, who was getting a little giddy, clutched hold of his hair with both hands. Luckily there was plenty of hair to hold on to, bright ginger in colour.

'Why should a man from the British Museum come to look at a big round stone thing?'

'Because they think it's King Arthur's Round Table, that's why!'

Sandy shot off down a path, did a circle round two trees, and came back the same way that he had gone.

'What makes them think that?' asked Arabel, holding on even tighter, and ducking her head, as they passed under some trees with low branches.

'Because there's a long sword stuck right in the middle of the stone table. And it has a red sparkling ruby in the handle. And they think it might be King Arthur's sword *Excalibur*!'

Arabel had never heard of King Arthur's sword *Excalibur*, and she was beginning to feel rather unwell. The tomato soup, the battered fish fingers, and the banana that she had eaten for her lunch had all been whizzed round inside her until her stomach felt like a spin dryer full of mixed laundry.

'I think I'd better get down now, Sandy,' she said politely. 'Thank you very much for the ride, but I'd better see what Mortimer is doing.'

'OK,' said Sandy, and he glided to a stop beside a tree, holding his arm round the trunk as he came up to it. Then he lifted Arabel off his shoulders and put her down on the ground. Arabel found that her legs would not hold her up, and she sat down, quite suddenly, on the grass. Her head still seemed to be whirling round, even though she was sitting still.

'I do feel funny,' she said.

'You'll be better in a minute,' said Sandy, who was used to the feeling.

Arabel tried to look around her for Mortimer, but all the trees and people and grass and daffodils seemed to be swinging round in a circle, and she had to shut her eyes.

'Can you see Mortimer anywhere, Sandy?' she asked, with her eyes shut.

But Sandy had got back on to his wheel and pedalled away; he was juggling with his three balls as he rode.

Meanwhile, where *was* Mortimer?

He was still walking slowly and purposefully towards the LawnSabre, which Mr Walpole had left parked just beside the little hut in the middle of the garden where he kept his tools.

In order to reach the LawnSabre, Mortimer had to cross the paved area where the skaters were gliding about on their skateboards.

'Watch out!' yelled a boy, whizzing past Mortimer on one wheel. Mortimer jumped backwards, and two other skaters nearly collided as they tried to avoid him. Three more skaters shot off the pavement and ended up in a bed of daffodils.

'You mind out for my daffs, or I'll report ye to the Borough!' bawled old Mr Walpole angrily. He had been walking towards the tool shed to put away the LawnSabre, but now he stepped into the flower bed, and began indignantly straightening up the bent daffodils, and tying them to sticks, shaking his fist at the skaters.

Mortimer, taking no notice of what was happening behind him, stepped off the pavement, and walked on to where the LawnSabre was standing.

The LawnSabre was bright red. It was mounted on four smallish wheels, and it had a pair of long handles, like a wheelbarrow, and a switch for the fuel, and a lever to raise or lower the blades (so as to cut the grass long or short). At present, the lever was lowered, so that the blades would cut the grass as short as possible.

The motor had to be started by pulling a string; as Mortimer already knew, from watching Mr Walpole through the window.

The switch for the fuel was already switched to the ON position. Mr Walpole had left it that way when he went off to talk to Mr Dunnage.

Meanwhile Arabel was beginning to feel a little better, and she was able to open her eyes. She looked around her for Mortimer, but could not see him anywhere. She stood up, holding on to a tree to balance herself, because the ground still seemed to be rocking about under her feet. She could see Sandy in the distance; he was now pedalling about, holding an open umbrella in one hand, and a top hat in the other; he waved the top hat to Arabel, and then put it on his head.

'Sandy, have you seen Mortimer?' called Arabel, but Sandy did not hear her.

'Are you feeling all right, my dear?' said a lady in a blue hat, walking up to Arabel. 'You look rather green.'

'Yes, thank you, I'm all right,' said Arabel politely. 'But I am anxious about my raven, Mortimer. I would like to find him. Have you seen him, please?'

'Your raven?' said the lady. 'I'm afraid, my dear, that you are still a little bit dizzy. You had better sit by me quietly on this seat for a while. Then we will look for your mummy. I am rather surprised that she let you do that dangerous ride on that boy's shoulders.'

The lady obliged Arabel to sit beside her on a bench; she held on to Arabel's hand very tightly.

'Now tell me, my dear,' she said, looking round the garden, 'what sort of clothes is your mummy wearing? Is she a tall lady or a short one? Does she have a hat and coat on?'

'She has an overall covered with flowers,' said Arabel. 'But –'

Taking no notice of Arabel, the lady began stopping people as they passed by, and saying: 'This little girl seems to have lost her mummy. Will you tell her, if you see her, that I have her child, and am sitting on this bench?'

'Excuse me,' said Arabel politely. 'It isn't my mother that I have lost, but my raven, Mortimer. He doesn't have a coat, but he is quite tall, for a raven. And he is black all over and has hair on his beak.'

'Oh dear,' said the lady, 'I am afraid you are still feeling unwell, my poor child. Perhaps we had better look for a nice, kind policeman. I am sure *he* will be able to take you to your mummy, who must be very worried, wondering where you have got to.'

By this time Mortimer had climbed up on top of the LawnSabre, and had found the string that was used to start the motor. He took firm hold of it in his strong hairy beak.

Mr Walpole was still crossly propping up his battered daffodils and tying them to sticks with bits of raffia which he took out of his trouser pocket. He did not notice what Mortimer was doing.

'Are you feeling a little better now, my dear?' said the lady in the blue hat.

'Yes, thank you,' said Arabel, at last managing to wriggle loose from the lady's grasp. And she climbed down from the bench.

'Then,' said the lady, grabbing Arabel's hand again, 'we will go and find a nice, kind policeman.'

'But I don't want a policeman,' said Arabel. 'I want my raven, Mortimer.'

Just at that moment Mortimer gave the cord of the LawnSabre a tremendous jerk. The motor, which was still warm, burst at once into an ear-splitting roar.

'Kaaark!' shouted Mortimer joyfully.

'Hey!' shouted old Mr Walpole, looking round from his broken daffodils. 'Who the pest has started my mower? Hey, you! You get away from that-urr machine. Don't you dare start it!'

But it was too late. Mortimer jumped from the starting-string to the right handle of the LawnSabre. There was a switch on the handle which had four different positions: START, SLOW, FAST, and VERY FAST. Mortimer's jump shifted the switch from the START to the FAST position, and the mower began rolling over the grass.

'Oh, my goodness!' said Arabel. *'There's* Mortimer!'

And, pulling her hand out of the lady's clasp, she began running towards Mortimer and the LawnSabre, as fast as she could go. The LawnSabre, at the same time, was rolling equally fast towards Arabel.

'NEVERMORE!' yelled Mortimer, mad with excitement, jumping up and down on the handle of the mower. His jumping moved the lever into the VERY FAST position, and the LawnSabre began to go almost as quickly as Sandy on his wheel, or the skaters on their skateboards, careering across the grass towards Arabel.

'You there! You stop that mower directly, do you hear me?' shouted Mr Walpole.

But Mortimer did *not* hear Mr Walpole – the LawnSabre was making far too much noise for him to be able to hear anything else at all. Even if Mortimer *had* heard Mr Walpole, he would not have paid the least attention to him. Mortimer was having a wonderful time. The LawnSabre crashed through a bed of daffodils and tulips, mowing them as flat as a bathmat.

Mr Walpole let out a bellow of rage. 'Stop that, you black monster!' he shouted. 'You bring that-urr mower back here!'

But Mortimer did not have the least intention of stopping the LawnSabre. And, even if he had meant to, he did not know how to stop the motor.

The LawnSabre went on racing across a stretch of grass which had already been cut once, and then it crossed the paved strip where the skaters were skating. The noise made by the metal blades on the stone pavement was dreadful – like a giant mincer grinding up a trainload of rocks.

'Oh, my blades!' moaned Mr Walpole, putting his hands over his ears.

Now Mortimer noticed Arabel running towards him.

With a loud shriek of pride and enjoyment, he drove the LawnSabre straight in her direction.

'WATCH OUT!' everybody shouted in horror. Mr Walpole turned as white as one of his own snowdrops, and shut his eyes. The kind lady in the blue hat fainted dead away, into a bed of pink tulips. For it seemed certain that the LawnSabre would run over Arabel and mow her as flat as the daffodils.

But just then, luckily, Sandy, who had seen what was happening from the other side of the garden, came pedalling over the grass at frantic speed on his wheel. He swung round in a swooping curve, and just managed to catch up Arabel in his umbrella and whisk her out of the way of the LawnSabre as it chewed its way along.

'Oh, WELL DONE!' everybody shouted.

Mr Walpole opened his eyes again.

Sandy and Arabel had crashed into a lilac bush, all tangled up with each other and the wheel and the umbrella, but they were not hurt. As soon as Arabel had managed to scramble out of the

bush, she went running after Mortimer and the LawnSabre.

'Stop him, oh please stop him!' she panted. 'Can't somebody stop him? Please! It's Mortimer, my raven!'

'All very well to say stop him, but how's a body a-going to set about that?' demanded Mr Walpole. 'That-urr mower's still got half a tank o'fuel in her; her'll run for a good half-hour yet, and dear knows where that feathered fiend'll get to in that time; he could mow his way across half London and flatten the Houses o' Parliament 'afore anybody could lay a-holt of him. What we

need is a helicopter, and a grappling iron, and a posy o' motorcycle cops.'

But before any of these things could be fetched, it became plain that the headlong course of the LawnSabre was likely to end in a very sudden and drastic manner. For Mortimer and the mower were now whizzing at breakneck speed straight for the huge crater at the bottom of which the round stone table with the sword in it had been discovered.

'Nevermore!' shouted Mortimer, looking ahead joyfully, and remembering the jet plane he had seen take off into the air at Heathrow.

Arabel, running after him across the grass, was now much too far behind to have any hope of catching up.

'Mortimer!' she panted. 'Please turn round. Please come back! Can't you stop the motor?'

But Mortimer could not hear her, and anyway he did not wish to turn or stop. With a final burst of speed, the LawnSabre shot clean over the edge of the huge hole, breaking through the guard fence as if it had been made of soapsuds.

A scream of horror went up from all the people in the garden. And the people who were down in

the bottom of the hole suddenly saw a large red motor mower in mid-air right over their heads, with Mortimer sitting on it.

Luckily there was just time for them to jump back against the sides of the hole.

Then the LawnSabre struck the stone table at the bottom of the hole. There was a tremendous crash; the sound was so loud that it could be heard all over Rumbury Town, from the cricket ground to the pumping station.

The LawnSabre was smashed to smithereens. The round stone table was crushed to powdery rubble.

But Mortimer, discovering with great disgust that the LawnSabre was not going to take off into the air as he had expected it would, had spread his wings at the last moment, and rose up into the air himself. He did not like flying, but there were times when he had to, and this was one of them.

So all the people up above in Rainwater Crescent Garden, who had rushed to the side of the hole in the expectation of seeing some dreadful calamity, were amazed to see a large black bird come flapping slowly up out of the crater, carrying a massive metal blade with a red flashing stone in the handle at one end.

As he rose up, Mortimer had grabbed at the hilt of the sword which had been stuck in the stone table; and he took it with him in his flight.

'Oh, if only I had brought my camera!' lamented Dick Otter, a young man from the Rumbury Borough News, who had come along because there was a rumour that King Arthur and all his knights had turned up in Rainwater Crescent.

Mortimer was feeling very ruffled. He wanted his tea. Also he did not quite know what to do with the metal blade he had brought up with him out of the hole. It was very heavy, and tasted disagreeably of old lettuce leaves left to soak too long in vinegar. Mortimer hated the feel of it in his beak. But he did like the red sparkling stone in the handle. He wanted to show it to Arabel.

Just at that moment Mr Dunnage the history teacher came rushing back with a white-bearded man, who was his friend Professor Lloyd-Williams from the British Museum, an expert in Arthurian history.

The first thing they saw as they ran into Rainwater Crescent Garden, was an open-mouthed, gaping crowd, all gazing up at a rope that was stretched like a clothes line between two plane trees.

And on this rope a large black bird was walking slowly along, swaying a good deal from side to side. In his beak he held a long, heavy-looking, rusty sword, with a red stone in its hilt.

'Oh dear,' said Mr Dunnage. 'That looks like the sword that was stuck in the table. But how in the world did that bird get hold of it?'

'Well now, indeed,' said Professor Lloyd-Williams, 'that certainly does look like the sword Excalibur; for a bardic description says that it was 'longer than three men's arms, with a three-edged blade, and three red rubies in the hilt'.'

'There's only one red stone,' pointed out Mr Dunnage.

'The others might have fallen out,' said the professor. 'And the bird, no doubt, is one of the Ravens of Owain, who were supposed to have set upon King Arthur's warriors in battle –'

'How the deuce are we going to get the sword *away* from the bird?' said Mr Dunnage.

Dick Otter, coming up to the two men, said, 'Oh, sir, if the sword really is King Arthur's sword Excalibur, can you say what it would be worth?'

'How can I tell?' said Professor Lloyd-Williams. 'It is unique. Perhaps a hundred thousand pounds. Perhaps a million.'

At this moment Arabel discovered where Mortimer had got to, and standing by one of the plane trees to which the rope was tied, she called, 'Mortimer! Mortimer? Please, I think you had better come down from there!'

By now Mortimer had walked about halfway across the rope, but he was nothing like so good

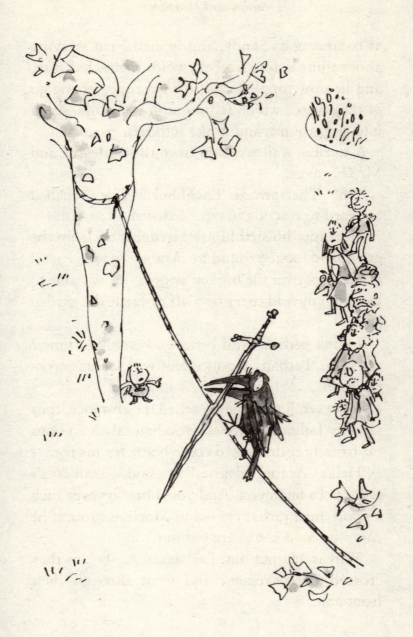

at balancing as Sandy, and he had been swaying about quite a lot. Arabel's voice distracted him, and he now toppled right off the rope, letting go of the sword, which fell point downwards, stuck into the ground, and broke into four pieces.

A terrible wail went up from the professor and Mr Dunnage.

'Oh! The sword Excalibur!' They rushed forward to rescue the bits of sword.

Mortimer hoisted himself irritably up from the grass, and looked round for Arabel. In the general excitement over the broken sword, she was able to pick him up and carry him off towards the garden gate.

'I think perhaps we'd better go home, Mortimer,' she said. 'Perhaps a policeman will see us across the road.'

However, just as they reached the entrance, they saw her father, Mr Jones, who had taken an hour off from taxi-driving to come home for his tea.

'Hello, Arabel, dearie,' he said. 'Your ma's sent me to fetch you. And you'd best be ever such a good quiet girl at tea – and Mortimer too, if he *can* – because she's rare put out.'

'Why is Ma put out, Pa?' asked Arabel, as they crossed the pavement and went through their front gate.

'Because Granny Jones phoned to say she's got a sore throat and she's not coming after all. Seems your Ma had just finished making you a new pink dress.'

Arabel was sorry that Granny Jones was not coming, but very glad that she did not have to wear the pink dress.

'It's lucky Ma doesn't know about your driving the LawnSabre, Mortimer,' she said, as she went up to the bathroom to wash her hands before tea. 'I don't think she'd have liked that.'

'Kaaark,' said Mortimer, who had almost forgotten about the LawnSabre, and was thinking about jam tarts, hoping very much that there would be some for tea. He lifted one of his wings, which felt fidgety, and shook it. Out from under his wing fell the red shining stone from the hilt of King Arthur's sword. It dropped into the washbasin, rolled around with the soapy water, and went down the plughole.

Extra!

Extra!

READ ALL ABOUT IT!

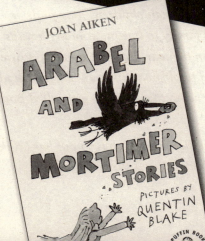

JOAN AIKEN

ARABEL AND MORTIMER STORIES

PICTURES BY QUENTIN BLAKE

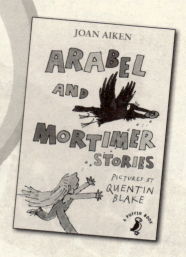

1924   Born 4 September in a haunted house on Mermaid
Street, Rye, East Sussex

1936   Joan goes away to boarding school age 12,
after being taught at home for many years

1940   Joan has a series of wartime jobs, meanwhile
writing lots of stories. She sends one in to the BBC
for their radio programme, Children's Hour, and
has it accepted!

1953   Married with two small children, Joan finds an
old bus for the family to live in, as many houses
were bombed in the war. Her first book of stories
is accepted and published this year. She has an idea
for an exciting adventure about a girl called Bonnie
Green . . .

1955   Joan's husband dies, and she has to put her book
aside and go to work for a story magazine

1962 *Finally completed, that book about Bonnie is published as* The Wolves of Willoughby Chase. *It is a great success, so at last Joan is able to work from home as a full time writer*

1967 *Joan begins to meet many of her readers through the Puffin Book Club, with Puffin making a film about her life and story ideas. You can see the film on her website* www.joanaiken.com

1969 *Joan receives the Guardian Award for* The Whispering Mountain *and* The Wolves *series, as well as the Lewis Carroll Award for* The Wolves of Willoughby Chase

1972 *Joan creates a new series about a girl called Arabel and her unbelievably crazy pet raven – Mortimer – and the stories appear on CBBC's* Jackanory *with drawings by Quentin Blake*

1981 *Asked to write a guide for would be children's authors, Joan produces a book called* The Way to Write for Children, *and dedicates it to her friend Kaye Webb, the editor of Puffin Books*

1989 *The film of* The Wolves of Willoughby Chase *is released; it was filmed in Poland where there was more snow!*

1991 *Joan works with Quentin Blake again on a collection of stories called* The Winter Sleepwalker. *By now she has written over eighty*

books including ten books in the Wolves Chronicles *series . . .*

1996   Black Hearts in Battersea, *the sequel to* Wolves *is filmed and shown on BBC TV*

1999   *Joan is presented with an MBE from the Queen for her contribution to children's literature*

2004   *Joan completes* The Wolves *series and dies on 4th January at the age of 79*

INTERESTING FACTS

There were more than a dozen Arabel and Mortimer stories shown on the BBC Jackanory programme. Some of Joan Aiken's amazing ideas were actually taken from real life! She and her brother rescued an owl they saw staggering down a country road which must have been bumped by a car. They wrapped it in a jacket and lifted it into the hedge to recover.

Another true story was about the small son of a friend who had become totally attached to a tie of his father's; it had to be kept in the fridge in case he needed it to get to sleep on a hot night – you will recognize both of these stories!

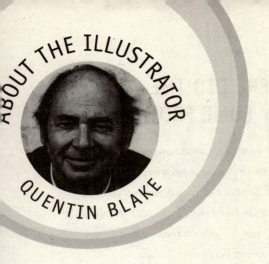

Quentin Blake has illustrated more than three hundred books, including all of the stories by Roald Dahl. In 1980 he won the prestigious Kate Greenaway Medal. In 1999 he became the first ever Children's Laureate and in 2013 he was knighted for services to illustration.

Quentin Blake and Joan Aiken enjoyed many years of collaboration on the Arabel and Mortimer stories. Quentin was an enthusiastic supporter of Joan's work, and his pictures are now inseparable from her characters. When the BBC came up with the idea of doing a 'Mortimer' puppet series he sent her a letter with a lovely idea on the back of the envelope:

WHERE DID THE STORY COME FROM?

Two of Joan Aiken's favourite authors directly inspired her to write about a mischievous raven. Charles Dickens kept a pet raven for his children which was very badly behaved; he wrote about this only-just-tame raven, which was called Grip, in his novel Barnaby Rudge.

On a lecture tour of America, Dickens met the writer Edgar Allan Poe who saw a portrait of Dickens' children and their raven, and was inspired to write his famous poem about the ghostly Raven who appeared to haunt him in his room one night, and would only utter one word: 'Nevermore!'

In 1972 Joan Aiken won an award, called an Edgar, for the best Young Adult spooky story of the year – her prize was a china bust of the poet. Both these literary ravens inspired her to write about her own mischievous bird – she considered many names for him, but finally decided to call him Mortimer.

GUESS WHO?

A '. . . walked – he never hopped – very slowly through into the hall and looked at the stairs. They seemed to interest him greatly.'

B '. . . was more than upset, she was in despair. She wandered about the house all day, looking at the things that reminded her of Mortimer.'

C 'He had packed himself tightly into the laundry basket and pulled the lid down over his head.'

D 'In the front hall he found a tartan shopping bag containing two raspberry dairy bricks, some electric light bulbs, and a head of celery.'

WORDS GLORIOUS WORDS!

*We often come across **new** or **unfamiliar** words when we're reading. Lots of Joan Aiken's characters use words you will never have heard before – because she made them up herself – but usually you can guess what they might mean!*

Arabel's uncle Mr Gumbrell talks about some odd creatures like these:

> A *Socrates bird*
>
> a *cassodactyl*
>
> and *a pterowary.*

Mrs Jones often gets in a muddle about '*deadly cheese mambas*' and skateboards being banned by '*Act of Parking Lot*' but usually we get the idea . . .

And when her characters get excited they say all sorts of odd things.

Do you remember who said:

'*Oh, my dear cats alive!*'

Or:

'*What we need now is a helicopter and a grappling iron and a posy o' motorcycle cops.*'

Or:

'*Sail bonny boat like a bird in the air,*
Over the sea to Spain.
Oh what a riot of fun we'll share,
Out on the bounding main . . .'

Does this song of Brandy Brown's remind you of one you may already know? It goes to a well-known tune . . .

1. *Auntie Brenda in The Bread Bin*
2. *Mr Walpole the Park Keeper in The Sword Excalibur* 3. *Over the Sea to Skye*

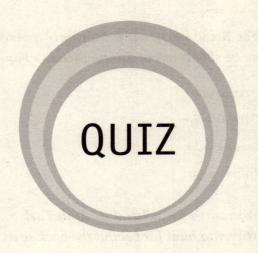

QUIZ

1 *In* Arabel's Raven, *Ebenezer Jones finds a bird. What is his first thought?*

a) *The bird is too noisy*

b) *The bird is dead*

c) *The bird is scary*

d) *The bird is asleep*

2 *In* The Escaped Black Mamba, *Mrs Jones thinks it's silly to have the phone where?*

a) *By the front door*

b) *In the bedroom*

c) *In the kitchen*

d) *Halfway up the stairs*

3 *In* **The Bread Bin,** *what is Mortimer covered in when he shoots out of Auntie Brenda's handbag?*

a) *Fizzy drink*

b) *Carrot peelings*

c) *Banana pulp*

d) *Breadcrumbs*

4 *In* **Mortimer's Tie,** *what does Arabel ask Mortimer to hunt for behind the back seat?*

a) *Diamonds*

b) *A tie*

c) *Keys*

d) *Prunes*

5 *In* **The Spiral Stair,** *who is in the same train carriage as Arabel and Mortimer?*

a) *A lady*

b) *Two gentlemen*

c) *A mother and her child*

d) *Nobody*

| 6 | *In* Mortimer and the Sword Excalibur, *what crashes through the flowerbeds?* |

a) *Children on skateboards*

b) *Sandy's unicycle*

c) *The LawnSabre*

d) *A digger*

IN
THIS YEAR

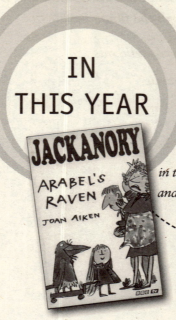

The most fashionable car is the brightly coloured Volkswagen 'Beetle'.

Lots of new shops and shopping centres open all over the country; the popularity of TV advertising explains Mrs Jones' passion for new gadgets.

In the 1970s, Barbie, Sindy and Action Man dolls become very popular.

Crazy UK fashions include 'hot pants' (shorts!) and bell-bottomed trousers; anything from cloaks and historical costumes to trouser-suits for girls become everyday wear.

In 1972 Britain switches to decimal currency. Before this there were 12 pence in a shilling, and 20 shillings in a pound. One coin worth two-and-a-half shillings, or 'two and six' was known as half a crown; the old 'crown', or five-shilling coin had been stopped in 1966.

In 1976, Concorde, the fastest passenger aeroplane in the world, comes into service.

The Walt Disney World Resort is opened in Florida.

The Clangers, The Magic Roundabout *and* Bagpuss *first appear on television.*

In 1977, the whole nation celebrates Queen Elizabeth's Silver Jubilee with street parties.

Watership Down *and* Charlie and the Great Glass Elevator *are published.*

MAKE AND DO

Mortimer is rather partial to Mrs Jones' jam tarts!
Why not try making some for tea.
(Always ask an adult to help you.)

YOU WILL NEED:

* 500g ready-made shortcrust pastry

* 12tsp jam (choose your favourite flavour)

* Plain flour, for sprinkling

* Rolling pin

* 12-hole tart tin

* A circle pastry cutter that is slightly larger than the holes in your tart tin

1 Preheat the oven to 180C (fan) / 350F / gas mark 4.

2 Lightly grease the tart tin with a little butter.

3 Sprinkle flour on a clean surface and roll out the pastry to the thickness of a £1 coin.

4 Using the pastry cutter, stamp out 12 circles and line the tin.

5 Prick each circle of pastry with a fork and spoon 1tsp of jam into each pastry case.

6 If you like, use the leftover pastry to cut out shapes and decorate the tarts.

7 Bake in the oven for 12–15 minutes, until the pastry is golden-brown.

8 Leave the tarts to cool on a wire rack.

9 Eat them before you-know-who gets his beak stuck in!

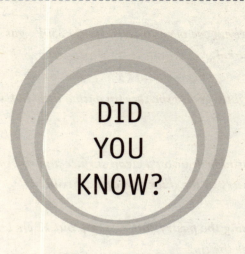

DID YOU KNOW?

The common raven is one of the most intelligent of all birds. It can communicate a wide range of messages through its call, and it can even imitate animal calls and human voices.

There are rare white ravens that are found in Canada – only a few are born each year.

A group of ravens is called an 'unkindness' or a 'conspiracy' because they are generally thought to be connected with bad luck or death.

Ravens have been part of many myths and legends throughout the ages. In some stories they are considered an omen of bad tidings. In Welsh myths, the raven is a bringer of death. Witches were believed to have the ability to change themselves into ravens to avoid capture. Native Americans often saw the raven as mischief-makers and in some tribes the bird is known as a stealer of souls. But ravens are also associated with Bible stories – the raven was the first bird Noah sent out from the ark to find land.

The origin of the ravens at the Tower of London is unknown, but eight birds are always kept there. The person in charge of the ravens is called the Ravenmaster.

Mortimer is mistaken for one of the ravens at the Tower of London in the BBC TV puppet series!

PUFFIN WRITING TIPS

Keep a travel journal when you go on holiday so you can capture all the exciting new sights and sounds.

Exercise! Go for a jog or even do some star jumps because once your blood starts pumping your mind will be racing!

From A–Z write a word that goes with every letter in the alphabet and then pick your favourite to write about.

FROM
THE
ARCHIVE

Joan Aiken would keep notes of funny ideas that might come in handy – even on the back of an old envelope!

Do you recognize any of these?

```
                    Arabel

      dog fetching toys out of his toy drawer

    man who eats veg in alphabetical order
    putting things in freezer for safe keeping - frozen tomatoes

    3-ft African green monkey dashing across motorway
    Man with leg in plaster (cd conceal stolen jewels in leg)
    boy kicking along umbrella handle
    notice in car: Instant Mess.service

    lady who lends out hats for occasions (such as Bk House garden party)

    Joneses' 25th wedding anniv

    The Voice - old boy who walks about Rumbury Town hearing instructions

    Mortimer inside spindryer in dry cleaners'

    Big builder's chimney for debris - M going down it
    house with old mine subsidence behind it - the devil's ballroom: 80ft hole
    man pushing gumboots along on a trolley

    mortimer falling into bath while Mr Jones in it

    Arabel's tree Goose
    Man + bear escaping simultaneously from prison/zoo
      He was hijacken who'd used bear to get out of Ruritania
          killed somebody? stole crown jewels?

        Bradpole, the Ruritanian bear
```

BBC TV MORTIMER AND ARABEL PUPPET SERIES

The Arabel and Mortimer stories first appeared on the BBC Jackanory *programme, where they were read aloud, accompanied by Quentin Blake's hilarious illustrations. When the BBC decided to turn the Jones family and their riotous raven into giant puppets a whole new world was created.*

Joan and her daughter Lizza wrote several new stories, including one where Mortimer goes to visit his Raven ancestors at the Tower of London, and is mistaken for a ghost! (See picture on page 357.)

Mortimer and the Jones family and their house in Rainwater Crescent all came to life, looking just like the Quentin Blake pictures – it was great fun to see Mortimer in action!

See more about the TV series and all the Mortimer stories on the Joan Aiken website: www.joanaiken.com